Hungarian Folk-tales

Retold and illustrated by
VAL BIRO

OXFORD UNIVERSITY PRESS
OXFORD   NEW YORK   TORONTO

Oxford University Press, Walton Street, Oxford OX2 6DP

Oxford New York Toronto
Delhi Bombay Calcutta Madras Karachi
Petaling Jaya Singapore Hong Kong Tokyo
Nairobi Dar es Salaam Cape Town
Melbourne Auckland

and associated companies in
Berlin Ibadan

Oxford is a trade mark of Oxford University Press

A CIP catalogue record for this book is available
from the British Library

ISBN 0 19 274148 9

Printed in Great Britain

Author's Note

I have adapted the stories in this book from Hungarian collections, notably those by Emil Kolozsvári Grandpierre and Gyula Illyés, whose books were compiled from various collections of regional folk-tales. The sources of those, in turn, can be traced back to the word-of-mouth tradition of peasant story-tellers.

I am particularly indebted to my wife, Marie-Louise Biro, for her editorial work and also for her considerable help in the phraseology of these narratives.

Contents

To the memory of my mother

The Thieving Goblins

THERE was once a poor man who had so many children that he was never able to count them for sure. Sometimes he thought that he had about fifty, at other times there only seemed to be about fifteen.

The fact remained that a crowd like that required a mountain of food and the poor man was quite unable to provide it. One day, therefore, he decided to send a dozen of them into service so that the rest could at least have enough to live on.

He asked his children to form two ranks and he began to

count them. There were twelve in the front rank, he found. Twelve! Therefore, he concluded at last, he must have twenty-four children in all! Now then, he wondered, which of the two rows should be sent into service? He had a lucky penny. Heads for the front row, tails for the back. He spun. Tails. Seeing this the poor man promptly broke into tears, because the back row contained his youngest son Georgie.

'Never mind, dear father,' said Georgie, 'I am strong enough to do any kind of work!'

'Very well,' said he, 'but here is my lucky penny to bring you good fortune.' And he gave it to him.

'Thank you father,' said Georgie, 'and if the lucky penny isn't much help to me, I will try to be of some help to it: that way we shall always remain good friends.'

So, one fine day, the twelve brothers from the back row set out to seek employment, and they travelled for a day and a night.

The following morning Georgie noticed a dot in the distance. As they got nearer he saw that it wasn't a dot any more, but a big castle. And not just an ordinary castle either, but a spinning castle! It stood on a single red cockerel's leg on which it spun round like a top.

'We may well find employment here,' said the brothers, 'but who on earth could get into a spinning place like that?'

'I shall find a way,' said Georgie. He produced his lucky penny and took good aim at the cockerel's leg. The penny found its target with a clang and, at that precise moment, the castle stopped its dizzy spinning. Each of its forty-eight doors opened at the same time, and from each door twenty-four armed soldiers rushed forth. They grabbed the twelve brothers and dragged them in front of the Black King.

The King was sitting on a black throne. Behind the throne stood a Princess, and she was eating popcorn.

'How dare you stop my castle?' demanded the King angrily.

Georgie knew that his brothers were too frightened to answer, so he stepped forward boldly, saluted smartly, and announced:

'Your Majesty, I place my life in your hands, but do not harm my brothers. It was I who stopped your castle!'

The King was so surprised that his pipe dropped out of his mouth.

'Are the twelve of you all the children of one father?'

'Most certainly, Your Majesty,' replied Georgie.

'An able man, your father,' nodded the King appreciatively.

'Twice as able as Your Majesty thinks — we have twelve more brothers at home,' boasted Georgie.

'Hm,' mused the King. 'And despite my kingly status I have no more than one single granddaughter.'

'That's not a lot,' admitted Georgie and looked at the Princess. She looked at Georgie — and what she saw pleased her so much that she swallowed an entire handful of popcorn in one go.

The King, thereupon, engaged the twelve brothers as herdsmen to look after the royal stud, and took them down to the stables. The brothers were astounded. The stable was as big as a town and it housed no less than twelve hundred golden-haired horses who were munching hay out of diamond mangers.

'Now follow me to the castle wall,' ordered the King. What the brothers saw sticking up from the battlements was a grim row of stakes. .

'Are you trying to frighten us, Your Majesty?' enquired Georgie.

'Precisely,' said the King. 'Herdsmen go to those stakes if a single golden horse of mine goes missing! BUT, if my herd remains intact for the next three days and nights, I shall reward you. You, Georgie, will receive my grand-daughter in marriage, with half my kingdom, your brothers will become Earls. But for now, go and take my horses out to graze.'

The twelve brothers gathered a hundred horses each and drove them out to the meadow. Georgie and his hundred were last to leave the stable, and outside the gates he noticed a thin little horse, standing forlornly by the ditch at the roadside.

Georgie's heart went out to the poor little creature. He crossed over to stroke him gently.

'What ails you, my poor fellow?' he asked.

The little horse spoke:

'The previous herdsmen used to take their tempers out on me, and they always beat me mercilessly.'

'Don't be afraid of me,' encouraged Georgie, 'I won't hurt you. Tell you what, come out to the meadow with me and I'll play with you.'

A crowd of villagers was watching as the brothers drove out their herds.

'What a crying shame!' they lamented. 'Such handsome young lads, and to think they'll all end up on the stakes!'

Out in the meadow, the brothers were bewildered: what danger could they be facing? Was it from thieves?

The little horse whispered in Georgie's ear:

'Yes, but not ordinary ones. These are thieving goblins and they are after the King's horses!'

Georgie squared his shoulders and announced that he was not afraid of any goblin in the world.

'And you need have no fear either,' replied the little horse, 'if you have pipes with you!'

'But we have no pipes,' said Georgie.

'Then you must quickly borrow some from the King. He has a cartful of them. Let us go and see him now.'

Georgie hadn't the faintest idea how any man could fight goblins with pipes, but he trusted the little horse and mounted him just the same. The little horse shook himself and shot straight up into the air. In the twinkling of an eye they were above the castle and they dropped down straight in front of the King.

He was so alarmed that he nearly swallowed his tongue.

'How on earth did you drop in?' he enquired, recovering a little.

'From the sky. I usually fly when I am on urgent business,' replied Georgie proudly. He then asked the King for twelve good pipes. The King was still a little dazed, but sent his butler to fetch them without asking further questions. The pipes were of the finest, except that they had very long stems: the shortest of them was longer than Georgie.

They returned to the meadow before you could turn round. Georgie took the pipes and placed one in the mouth of each of his brothers.

'What about the tobacco?' they enquired.

The little horse whispered to Georgie:

'You don't need real tobacco. Elder leaves will do, and there's plenty of that here in the meadow.'

The brothers went to gather some leaves. They denuded half-a-dozen elders so vigorously that the trees were puzzled how autumn had come so soon.

The twelve boys sat down to practise their pipe-smoking and, before long, they were quite dizzy and green in the face.

'Put your pipes down for the present,' said the little horse. 'I will tell you when to smoke.'

The brothers were indignant. 'We have pipes, so we smoke,' said the eleventh brother. 'Anyway, why should we listen to a mere horse?'

The little horse felt that he must make some gesture to emphasize the urgency of the matter. So he jumped up from where he stood into a cloud overhead and then dropped gently back again.

'Perhaps now you will listen to me! I mean to help you. You must know that precisely at midnight, twelve goblins will appear. Should these goblins breathe on you, you will immediately fall asleep. All the previous herdsmen went to sleep and their herds were stolen by the goblins. But you need have no fear if you just blow your elder-leaf smoke into their eyes.'

The brothers calmed down on hearing this and put their pipes down. They didn't touch them again until the little horse warned:

'The goblins are coming!'

The brothers sprang up and ran to their herds, each with a pipe in his mouth. They puffed away bravely. The goblins breathed their sleepyfying breaths until their lungs nearly burst. They must have been amazed that the herdsmen weren't asleep, but, on the contrary, very much awake. And when a goblin so much as touched a horse, he got a smart rap on his knuckles. They fought for an hour, the goblins with their breaths, the herdsmen with elder-leaf smoke. Eventually, the goblins lost their strength in the smoke and retreated in shame.

'Your Majesty,' announced Georgie next day, saluting the King, 'your herds are safe and sound!'

'I know,' answered the King, 'because I saw them from here. But don't be too confident – there are two more nights to come.'

Next day the brothers drove their herds to the meadow again.

That evening the little horse left his grazing and came to see Georgie.

'I hear that the Queen of the Goblins is angry,' he said. 'She is sending a hundred goblins against us tonight.'

'That's a lot of goblins,' said Georgie.

'Don't worry,' said the little horse, 'there is quite enough elder in this meadow. Go and gather enough of it to build twelve bonfires, one for each of your herds.'

The brothers built twelve tall bonfires and lit them at ten o'clock. Black smoke billowed up, covering the whole meadow.

The thieving goblins arrived at midnight in a mighty swishing of wings and flew straight into the smoke. Their eyes smarted, they coughed and sneezed, whined and screeched, but tried to advance just the same towards the horses. They couldn't see a thing. Neither could the boys as they cracked their whips blindly to frighten the goblins. More than once a goblin was heard to wince when a whip had hit its mark. But the horses were unharmed and, after a good hour's fighting, the goblins retreated again in exasperation.

The Queen of the Goblins was even more exasperated. She was determined to get those horses! She decided to lead the entire goblin army herself next night.

The King saw for himself next morning that his herds were still intact, but it didn't make him happy. He was muttering to himself and scratching his head. It is a well-known fact that kings mutter when they are angry and scratch their heads when they are thinking. Therefore, this King was angry and he was thinking. But only the little horse noticed all this.

He rubbed himself against Georgie.

'You must get to work at once,' he urged, 'and build a hundred bonfires today. My itchy left ear tells me that the Queen of the Goblins is furious and there will be a great battle tonight.'

The brothers worked with a will and there wasn't a single elder bush left in the meadow. Tremendous bonfires towered all over it instead.

Whilst the twelve brothers took a well-earned rest from their labours the little horse sidled up to Georgie again:

'Have you still got your lucky penny?' he asked.

When Georgie said he had, the horse gave him another penny.

'Keep this in your left-hand pocket, and should the Princess ask for your lucky penny, give her mine instead.'

Georgie could not imagine why she should ask for a penny when she had gold and silver by the barrel.

'Because the King will order it,' explained the horse. 'He now regrets his promise of the Princess to you, along with half his kingdom. He much prefers the Red Prince to whom he has offered the whole of his kingdom this very day, if he accepts to marry the Princess. What is more, he told her to wheedle your lucky penny out of you because without it you will never be able to enter the castle again!'

'But a promise is a promise!' bridled Georgie. 'Be he King a hundred times over, I demand my rights!'

There was no time for more and the herdsmen lit the bonfires. The fires blazed so brightly and the elder-smoke billowed so darkly that the whole village crowded round to see the sight. Presently, they had to make way for a golden coach in which the King himself and the Princess came to watch the battle.

Precisely at midnight the little horse called out:

'The goblins are coming!'

They came by the thousand. Half the sky was blotted

out by their hordes and, in their midst, floated the Queen of the Goblins' coach drawn by six winged horses. The King saw them and jumped up shaking his fists, because they were his very own horses! He shouted and cursed in such language that even his coachman blushed and had to stop his ears.

The goblins swooped down with such menacing screeches that it looked as if nobody could ever withstand them. But when they plunged into the elder-smoke they started to cough and sneeze and splutter so violently that they nearly choked. Soon they were overcome by the fumes. There was then such a falling of goblins from the sky that even the oldest villagers couldn't remember ever seeing the like of it.

The herdsmen kept cracking their whips and the goblins kept tumbling down. The Queen of the Goblins herself fell down but rather more slowly because her billowing skirts helped to steady her.

The bonfires had hardly died down before the entire meadow was covered with goblins. If anybody had had a mind to walk the length and breadth of the district he could have done it on the backs of goblins — but nobody actually thought of trying. The herdsmen were busy tying them up because they knew that when the goblins recovered, their vengeance would be terrible.

Georgie marched up to the King and saluted smartly:

'Majesty, Sixthousandfivehundredandnineteen goblins, one Queen and six winged horses made prisoner. Royal herd of horses all present and correct. Sire!'

'At ease!' commanded the King. He blew a gold whistle, and a thousand armed soldiers appeared immediately. 'Take the prisoners to the castle and throw them into the dungeons!'

When the soldiers departed, the King produced a lead

whistle and blew that. In a flash the royal horse-doctor came running.

'Do you see those six winged horses?' he growled. 'They were stolen from me by that villainous Queen and she has disfigured them with those hideous wings. Cut them off!'

The horse-doctor did as he was commanded. The six pairs of wings were handed to the chambermaids of the Court who made twelve fans out of them, and they gave the best one to the Princess. She thanked them and spoke to Georgie:

'Would you like to have this pretty fan?'

'Yes, I would,' replied Georgie, 'even though you want my lucky penny in exchange.'

The Princess was astonished to see that Georgie knew her real purpose. She burst into tears:

'What can I do? My grandfather commanded me to obtain it from you. But I love you more than I love my grandfather, or my life. I won't take your penny even if they throw me into prison!'

'Don't worry, take it,' replied Georgie, giving her the little horse's bad penny, 'and leave the rest to me.'

When the King saw that the penny was safely in his granddaughter's hands he gave a signal and the royal coach shot away.

At dawn, the twelve brothers drove their herds back to the castle. It was spinning like a top, in a veritable whirlwind. One of its windows opened and the beautiful Princess looked out. Georgie greeted her in a respectful manner and she acknowledged his greeting with becoming modesty. Then she aimed the penny at him and threw it so skilfully that he caught it in mid-air. Just then the Red Prince appeared by her side.

'I will go and denounce you to your grandfather!' he threatened, as he slapped the Princess's snow-white hand.

'Don't bother,' she replied tartly, 'because I'll tell him myself. And I wouldn't marry you if you were the last man on earth!'

The Red Prince began to menace her in such a bullying way that Georgie thought it was high time to act. He produced his lucky penny and threw it with deadly accuracy at the cockerel's leg on which the castle spun. There was a clang and it stopped spinning at once. Georgie rushed in and up the steps. Coming towards him was the old King, with the Red Prince close behind. The King was in a bad mood and kept tugging at his pockets, turning them inside out.

'Your Majesty,' said Georgie in a loud voice, 'we have completed our service. The time has come for your promise to be fulfilled!'

The King started to cough as if he had swallowed something.

'Can't you see how old I am?'

Georgie certainly could. The King's face was a mass of wrinkles and he kept buckling at the knees.

'An old man's memory is like a sieve,' croaked the King. 'I must have forgotten my promise. Forgive me, my boy, but I have given my granddaughter to this Red Prince already.'

'Can you see how young I am, Your Majesty?' asked Georgie.

The King was bound to admit this whether he liked it or not.

'A young man's memory is sound,' continued Georgie. 'I remember your every word, Sire, and I shall not move until your promise to me and my brothers is fulfilled.'

This was too much for the Red Prince. He was purple in the face.

'I won't stand for this! I'll cut you down, along with your eleven brothers!' he cried and drew his sword. He snarled as if he wanted to taste blood by the bucket.

'Give me a sword, somebody!' Georgie shouted. But everybody in the castle was on the King's side and no one moved. So he snatched the old King's sword and beckoned to the Prince to come into the courtyard.

The Prince leapt on his charger and Georgie leapt on his little horse. They circled each other and joined battle. Their swords flashed. They crossed swords again and again. Suddenly, the Prince struck so hard that Georgie's sword broke in half. 'Aha!' gloated the Prince. 'I've got him now! I'll cut his head off!' He spurred his charger, but the little horse was prepared and, as the Prince struck, he leapt nimbly aside. The Prince lost his balance, flew out of the saddle and went sprawling to the ground like a toad.

Georgie leapt down and pointed his broken sword at the Prince's heart.

'I could kill you now,' he said. 'I know that you would have had no mercy on me. I won't kill you, but I order you to remove your carcass from this place and be gone for ever. Otherwise, I'll throw your carroty head to the pigs!'

The Red Prince crept away. He was so abashed that he went without a glance at the King, the Princess, or even at the least of the servants. And he has never been heard of since.

'I see now,' said the old King, 'that you understand the sword as well as you understand horses. In that case, I see no reason why you should not be able to learn about kingship as well. Suffice it to say that I give you the hand of my granddaughter and half my kingdom. Send for your father and the other twelve brothers because we shall have a feast.'

There was a feast all right. There were more doughnuts than stars in the sky, and there was more wine than water in the Danube. Georgie threw his lucky penny into the well so that it could have a well-earned rest, now that it had done its duty.

And the castle is still spinning round like a top because it stands on such a strong cockerel's leg. If you don't believe this, go and have a look for yourself one day!

Tobias and the Dragon

ONCE upon a time there was a poor man called Tobias.
He was so poor that he could hardly have been
poorer, yet every year he became poorer still. And
he became poorer each year because each year another baby
arrived. When there were more children in his house than
there are holes in a sieve, Tobias went out to seek work.
The work would earn him money and the money would
serve to buy bread for his huge family.

He walked and tramped for days until, one day, he came

to a wide field which belonged to a seven-headed dragon. No sooner had Tobias realized this but the dragon himself appeared, and stood in front of him belching flames from each of his seven mouths.

Tobias was afraid but he knew that he would not get far if he showed fear. So he pretended that he was not. Without waiting for the dragon to speak, he shouted in a menacing way:

'Why, you dirty dragon, what are *you* doing here?'

'What am *I* doing here?' asked the dragon, somewhat taken aback. 'If you must know, this field is mine!'

'Very well, then,' said Tobias. 'Let us have a contest. Whichever of us is the stronger, this field will belong to him. But, take care, you ragged dragon, I am fearfully strong!'

'Right,' said the dragon, 'let it be as you say. But what kind of a contest have you in mind?'

Tobias looked round and he saw a rock.

'Let's see what you can squeeze out of that rock,' he said, pointing to it.

Without a word the dragon broke off a piece of rock, rubbed it between his palms as if it were a snowball and then he began to squeeze. In no time at all the rock had crumbled into flour.

'Nice,' said Tobias, 'but I can do better than that. I will squeeze whey out of that rock!'

So saying, he got hold of another piece of rock, secretly took a piece of cheese out of his pocket and pressed them together. The dragon tasted the droplets and, sure enough, it *was* whey.

'Well,' said the dragon, impressed, 'if you are as strong as that let us be friends.'

'That's all right with me,' agreed Tobias, 'but only if you will regard me as your elder brother.'

The dragon agreed and they set out across the wide field, like brothers. By and by they reached a tree which was covered with an abundance of cherries.

'Let us eat!' cried the dragon.

'I would gladly eat,' thought Tobias, 'but I could never climb that tree to get at the cherries!' Then an idea struck him.

'You must pull down the top of the tree,' he told the dragon, 'and hold it until I have eaten my fill. When I have done, it will be your turn. After all I am your elder brother.'

The dragon did as he was bid, and Tobias ate his fill until his stomach was as round as a drum.

'Now you must hold the tree down for *me*,' said the dragon. But Tobias could not hold it down. Oh dear! As soon as the dragon let go, the tree straightened up again and that is how Tobias learnt to fly. When he had had enough of flying, the tree flung him straight into the middle of a bush, on top of a fat hare who was resting under it. They were both alarmed and the hare tried to run away. But he could not because Tobias was on top of him.

The dragon was wondering what Tobias was up to.

'Just this,' said Tobias, recovering quickly, 'that I saw this hare, I leapt over the cherry tree to make sure that he would not run away and, see here, I caught him too!'

The dragon was so impressed by this hare-catching that he invited Tobias to come to his village. They arrived by nightfall and found the family at supper. Four of them were sitting round the table, father, mother and two brothers, and each of them had seven plates on the table. Because each of them was a seven-headed dragon. Twenty-eight pairs of eyes fixed on Tobias as he came in and they stared in silence until father dragon asked:

'Why did you bring this rubbishy man to our house?'

'Speak with respect of my friend here,' replied the dragon, 'because however rubbishy, he is so strong that if you annoy him, he might eat us all up in his anger!'

'If he is your friend we welcome him,' said father dragon and showed Tobias where to sit. Mother dragon placed a plate in front of Tobias and he began to eat. The poor man only had one head but he was so hungry that with one head he ate more than the dragons with their seven each.

Neither did he do much else at the dragon's house but eat and sleep. He would wake up in the morning, wash a little and then begin to have breakfast. He would go on eating, nice and slow, until the midday bells sounded. By then it was not worth leaving the table because lunch was brought in. He would eat his lunch without haste, eating away until nightfall and the sound of bells again, when supper was served. He ate until he became sleepy, and when he was sleepy he went to sleep, and while he slept he ate nothing. As soon as he woke up, though, he started to eat all over again.

The dragons had a custom of fetching water from a well, each in turn. They used a bucket for this: a huge bucket made out of the skins of twelve oxen. They were polite to their guest for a while, but as time passed, mother dragon one day spoke to Tobias:

'It's your turn to fetch the water today,' she said.

Tobias dragged himself to the huge bucket but he was so frightened of it that he dared not touch it at all. He could not have lifted it, anyway. He pondered what to do next, when a thought struck him.

'Come,' he told the dragon, 'and show me where the well is, so that I may fetch the water.'

'Shoulder the bucket, then,' replied the dragon, 'and I will show you.'

'Yes, yes,' replied Tobias cunningly. 'But if I shoulder the bucket I will not see the road and I will not find my way home.'

So the dragon took the bucket and led the way to the well. It was a big well and the dragons of seven villages took water from it.

When they arrived at the well, Tobias took a spade and started to dig a trench all round it. The dragon gazed and gazed for a while and then asked:

'What are you doing?'

'I shall take this well home,' replied Tobias, 'so that we need not tire ourselves by fetching water each day!'

The dragon began to wail and cry and begged Tobias to leave the well where it was because it was used by the dragons of seven villages and if Tobias took it away, the most frightful war would follow!

Tobias made to hesitate for a while, then he threw the spade down and spoke to the dragon:

'Well, if you don't want me to take the well home, you had better bring the water yourself!'

'Willingly,' replied the dragon, and he filled the bucket and shouldered it.

'Just a moment,' said Tobias – and with that he sprang up and settled himself on top of the bucket. So it was that the dragon carried the full bucket on his shoulder, with Tobias sitting on top.

Next day, mother dragon sent them to fetch wood from the forest. The dragon got down to it, according to ancient dragon custom, and began to tear up the trees root and branch. Tobias pondered for a while and then a thought struck him. He had a rope with him which he had brought for carrying the wood, and now he began to surround the whole forest with it. The dragon asked:

'What are you doing?'

'I shall take the entire forest home with me,' replied
Tobias, 'so that we need not tire ourselves with fetching
wood each day!'

'Alas, alack!' wailed the dragon, 'do not even think of
that! The dragons of seven villages fetch wood from here,
and if you took the forest away, the most dreadful war
would follow!'

Tobias made to hesitate for a while, then he threw the
rope down and spoke to the dragon:

'Well, if you don't want me to take the forest home, you
had better carry the wood yourself!'

'Willingly,' said the dragon, but now he was becoming
very angry. As he went on tearing up the trees root and
branch, he kept on contemplating how best to end with
Tobias. He contemplated for so long that, by and by, it
was dark.

They decided to spend the night in the forest and made a
fire and lay down to sleep. The dragon had a coat which he
spread over himself; Tobias had a cloak in which to wrap
himself. When Tobias was asleep, the dragon pulled the
cloak off him and threw it into the lake. He thought that as
Tobias got stiffer and stiffer with cold during the night it
would be easier to deal with him.

Tobias slept and slept until the cold woke him up. As
soon as he saw his cloak floating on the lake he knew what
the dragon was about. Without a word, he pulled off the
dragon's coat and threw it on the fire. Then he went back
to sleep and slept until morning. In the morning he spoke
to the dragon:

'What has my cloak done to you that you should have
thrown it into the lake?'

With that he took his stick and struck at the dragon's
coat on the fire, and the coat instantly turned into a heap of
ashes.

'This will be your fate too,' he warned, 'if you don't fetch my cloak out of the lake!'

And he ground his teeth too, the more to frighten the dragon.

The dragon jumped into the lake, not so much as a dragon but as a small dog, to retrieve the cloak.

Then he roped up the wood, Tobias sat himself on top of it, the dragon shouldered it and carried it home, with Tobias on top.

They got home at midday and mother dragon was waiting for them at the gate. She was furious to see that her son was again carrying Tobias on his back and she told the dragon that she wanted a word with him. This is what she said:

'Get rid of your friend and get him out of this house, otherwise I shall not tolerate you here, either. What kind of a dragon do you think you are to slave for a miserable rubbishy man like that? He has been here a month and he has not done a stroke of work yet!'

The dragon scratched his head. He could not oppose his mother, however frightened he was of Tobias. In the end he decided to fight Tobias, come what may.

'Come,' he told Tobias, 'let us fight!'

'That's all right with me,' said Tobias, 'but what will you give me if I win?'

'A barrel of gold,' promised the dragon, 'but if I win, you must go home.'

'Very well, then, but on one condition. You shall say *how* we should fight, and I shall say *where* we should fight.'

'Good,' agreed the dragon. 'Let us fight with sticks.'

'Well, if we are to fight with sticks,' replied Tobias, 'then let's go and choose suitable sticks for ourselves. Having chosen them I shall announce where we are to fight.'

The dragon went and tore up a huge poplar which stood by the side of the ditch, broke off its branches and announced that he would fight with that. Tobias chose a sapling.

'And now, where are we to fight?' asked the dragon in a bloodthirsty manner.

'In the pigsty,' replied Tobias.

They entered the pigsty, first the dragon, then Tobias. Inside the narrow pigsty the dragon, with his seven heads, four feet and two wings could hardly stir, let alone fight. Tobias, on the other hand, thrashed the dragon with his sapling at will.

The dragon wailed and, with all his seven heads a-dizzied, he begged for mercy and promised to pay the barrel of gold because Tobias had won.

A little later he sat thinking again, how best to end with Tobias. He thought and thought, then he spoke:

'Let us have a sneezing competition, brother. If you sneeze best, you will have a barrel of gold, but if I sneeze best, you must go home!'

'Very well,' said Tobias.

With that they went into the dragon-house and the dragon took a deep breath. He sneezed so mightily that Tobias nearly stuck to the ceiling as the wind whirled him up. When he found his feet again, he began to walk round the room along the cracked walls and proceeded to stop the gaps in them with little bits of rag.

'What are you doing?' asked the dragon.

'I am just stopping up the holes,' replied Tobias.

'And why are you stopping up the holes?'

'So that they shouldn't let out my sneeze. If they do, the house won't collapse. And if the house doesn't collapse, how will you be able to tell that I sneezed best?'

The dragon fell to his knees and begged Tobias not to

sneeze the roof away from over their heads, their poor dragons' heads!

'Very well,' said Tobias, 'I shall not sneeze if you don't wish it. But I must have my barrel of gold!'

The dragon measured out the second barrel of gold, too, and said:

'In fighting and in sneezing you are the stronger. But let us see whose voice is stronger? If you shout the loudest you will have a barrel of gold, but if I shout the loudest, you must go home.'

'Let's shout, then,' agreed Tobias, 'but first let's go to the blacksmith.'

'By all means,' said the dragon, 'but why?'

'So that he can make an iron hoop for your head. For if he doesn't hoop your head carefully, it will crack apart like an egg from my shouting!'

The dragon was afraid for his head, he was afraid for all his seven heads, and he quickly measured out a third barrel of gold instead.

'I know now,' he said, 'that you are stronger than me in every way.'

'You should have known that before now,' said Tobias. 'But I see that I am a burden to your family. Take the three barrels of gold on your back and me on top of the barrels, and take me to my home in peace.'

The dragon was glad that at last he would be rid of Tobias.

He took the sack with the three barrels of gold on his back and he placed Tobias on top. With that, he started off at a trot towards Tobias's village. As he trotted along, so Tobias urged him on:

'Gee-up, horsey, gee-up!'

They went through seven villages and seven forests, and the people in those seven villages and forests saw Tobias riding on the back of a dragon. They whispered to each other:

'Look, there trots the dragon who has turned into a horse!'

They dared not speak out loud, because some of them were afraid of the dragon, and some of Tobias. So they contented themselves with whispers.

At last they arrived at Tobias's village. At the gate they shook hands and said their farewells in friendship. The dragon shed a few tears, however, because he had a sensitive soul.

On his way home, the dragon was thinking how amusing life had been with Tobias and how bored he would be when he got back alone to his big dragon-house. As he trudged on, wrapped in thought, suddenly he heard a laugh. He looked round, and saw a fox who was twitching with laughter, with tears in his eyes and his tail a-wagging. The dragon thought that he would like to share the joke, because he felt he could do with a laugh himself at that moment.

'What are you laughing at?' he asked the fox.

'At you, my dragon friend! Who else?'

'At me?' asked the dragon, perplexed. 'Why do you laugh at me?'

'Because you are the first dragon-turned-into-a-horse that I have ever seen in my life!'

'And who could have turned me into a horse?' objected the dragon. 'I am a dragon, and the best of dragons!'

The fox told him that it was Tobias who had turned him into a horse. By cheating him out of three barrels of gold when other men would never have dared to oppose a dragon, frightened as they were even of barking dogs. But that was nothing compared to the fact that Tobias had sat on the dragon's back and ridden him along the highway, like a horse.

The dragon thought this over and decided that if he had lost his honour, he could at least try to retrieve the three barrels of gold. He asked the fox for advice.

'Come back with me,' said the fox. 'For a cock and nine hens I will retrieve the gold for you.'

With that they turned back towards the village. Tobias saw them as they arrived at his gate. He knew that unless he thought of something quickly, he would never think of anything again, because the dragon would destroy him. A thought flashed through his mind. He shouted to the fox:

'You promised me nine dragon-skins! Do you mean to hoodwink me with this solitary dragon here?'

On hearing this, the dragon became so alarmed that he hit the fox over the head, ran away as fast as he could and never stopped until he got home.

As for Tobias, he built a palace with all his gold. He lives there still, with his ninety-nine children. And the dragons are still frightened of him, as if he had a dragon for breakfast every day!

A Donkey's Load

IT was neither here nor there, but somewhere in this wide world there was once a poor man. He lived at the edge of the village with his feeble and moulting old donkey.

One fine day he looked round his miserable shack for some food. But in vain: there wasn't even a single crust of dry bread in the place. So he drove his donkey out to the forest and loaded him up with a pile of wood. From forest to market. There he stood in a row with the other merchants and waited to sell his wood. A man, who looked like a barber, came up and asked:

37

'How much for that donkey's load, my man?'

The poor man named his price. The barber said it was too much and offered less; the poor man reduced his price a bit and finally they struck a bargain.

The poor man took up the halter and led his donkey to the barber's house. There he unloaded the wood and was about to leave with his donkey when the barber stopped him.

'Look here, my man, we struck a bargain on that donkey's load. And that includes the saddle too.'

The poor man protested, but the barber stuck to his guns. The saddle was his because he had paid for it. The poor man was unable to argue with him, so he unsaddled the donkey and trudged home.

But he was so angry that he couldn't rest. Of course he was angry: the barber had cheated him! And he was sorry about the saddle, too. He racked his brains. Then he had an idea. He took the donkey by the halter and didn't stop until he reached the barber's house. There he tied the donkey to the gatepost and entered the barber's shop. He greeted the barber and asked:

'How much for shaving me and my partner?'

The barber told him. The poor man paid accordingly and sat down. The barber shaved him well, then asked:

'And where's your partner?'

'He is just coming,' said the poor man. With that he went out, untied the donkey and led him back into the shop.

'Is that your partner?' asked the barber, appalled.

'Yes,' replied the poor man. 'I'll help you with the lathering.'

'You won't,' shouted the barber, 'I am no horse-barber and I won't shave donkeys!'

'I don't know what you are, sir, all I know is that we

struck a bargain and you accepted my money. There is nothing you can do but shave my partner. If you don't, I'll seek justice in the courtroom.'

The threat frightened the barber, so he tried to negotiate, offering to return the money and, on top of that, a brand-new razor, if only he were not asked to shave the donkey.

'I accept the brand-new razor,' replied the poor man, 'but only if you return my saddle as well, sir.'

What could the barber do but return the saddle? And ever since then the poor man does his own shaving.

Peter Cheater

ONCE upon a time there was a man called Peter. But everybody called him Peter Cheater because he was the biggest cheat and swindler this side of the seven seas. He liked a good joke, especially the kind of joke which took in fools who were only too easy to hoax, and there were plenty of those around: one born every minute! And if he made a little money on the side so much the better. In short, Peter enjoyed himself.

One day he happened to be strolling along the High

Street when whom should he meet but the respected Mayor of the town.

'Good morning, my man,' said the Mayor with a broad smile. 'We meet at last! I've been wondering about you for some time. They say that you are the biggest swindler in the world. Now then, do you think you could swindle me, too?'

'Why, certainly, Mr Mayor. The only trouble is that I need something for that, and I can't find it here.'

'Where can you find it, then?' asked the Mayor.

'Half-a-day's walk from here,' replied Peter Cheater.

'Well, my man, here's my horse, take it and fetch whatever you need. I am quite curious.'

So Peter took the horse and mounted it. He pretended that he couldn't ride, and sat on its neck for a while and then on its tail. People around laughed at the sight. Once out of the town, however, Peter rode properly, in fact just like a real hussar.

It was market day in a neighbouring village when Peter arrived there. A peasant accosted him and asked how much he wanted for his horse.

'With his tail, a thousand florins,' said Peter, 'without his tail a hundred.'

The peasant scratched his head. He could make no sense of this.

'Look,' explained Peter patiently, 'you can have the whole horse for a thousand. You can have him without his tail for a hundred. But if you want the tail only, give me nine hundred and the tail is yours!'

'In that case,' said the peasant, who wasn't born yesterday, 'I'd rather have the horse without the tail.'

'Done!' said Peter. He snipped off the tail, put it under his arm, pocketed the hundred florins, shook hands with the peasant and made himself scarce.

He didn't stop running, either, until he came to a pond outside the village. There, he waded in until he was waist deep, planted the horse's tail into the mud below, wedged it with a couple of heavy stones, smeared himself all over with the mud, came ashore and limped all the way back to the Mayor in great distress.

'Oh, Mr Mayor!' he lamented. 'What a calamity! You know I can't ride. The wretched horse bolted and took me straight into a pond! I was lucky to get out alive, but the poor beast has drowned!'

The Mayor, who had been laughing at Peter's woebegone appearance, stopped laughing at once. Instead he began to choke:

'You are a liar! I don't believe a word of it! You can't swindle me as easily as that!'

'Of course not!' said Peter pretending to be shocked. 'How could I swindle you? But if you don't believe me, respected Sir, please go and see for yourself. The horse's tail is still floating above the water. And if I don't speak the truth you can take me to the clink.'

The Mayor was reassured by Peter's polite words and calmed down.

'Very well, my man,' he said, 'lead me to the pond.'

Peter began to wail and lament once more. 'Oh dear, oh dear! How could I possibly go with you, Mr Mayor, with all my bones broken? I am more dead than alive!'

So the Mayor decided to go and see for himself. Sure enough, when he got to the pond the first thing he saw was the horse's tail still floating above the water. 'So Peter spoke the truth after all!' cried the Mayor. He was so pleased to see his horse's tail that he waded in straight away. Perhaps the poor beast hadn't yet drowned and he could pull it ashore! He grabbed the tail and pulled. He pulled with all his might until the two heavy stones gave way and splash! the Mayor went head over heels.

'The brigand!' he spluttered. 'He did take me in after all! He will pay for this! He'll go to the clink! He'll be put in irons!'

The Mayor went on spluttering and threatening – and all the while Peter Cheater was having a fine time at the inn with his friends. He had money in his pocket, after all. But when he looked out of the window and saw the Mayor coming along – covered in mud from head to foot and carrying a horse's tail in his hand, with two soldiers behind him – Peter realized he had to think fast.

'Landlord!' he called. 'Bring me five pints of wine, and here's the money. And whatever I do, just say that the wine has been paid for. Do you understand?'

The landlord did not really understand but, pocketing the money, he nodded eagerly that he did. And then the Mayor entered the bar parlour.

'Come in Sir, come in!' called out Peter welcomingly. 'Do take a seat with me!'

'I didn't come here to sit with you, my fine fellow!' spluttered the Mayor. 'I came here to arrest you and throw you into clink! My soldiers are outside. Pay for your drink and come at once!'

'Right away, Sir!' said Peter, obediently. He called the landlord. 'What do I owe you, landlord?'

The landlord played his part well. 'You had five pints earlier,' he said, 'and then another five. That makes ten pints if I am not mistaken.'

'Correct,' agreed Peter. With that, he took his hat off and threw it down. Looking at the landlord with a sly wink, he asked, 'Well, landlord, does this settle my bill?'

'It certainly does, sir!' he replied.

The Mayor stood amazed. He forgot all about the mud and the horse – though he was still holding the tail. He

looked at Peter, he looked at the landlord, he looked at the greasy hat on the floor.

'What kind of a hat's that, my man?' he asked.

'A very special kind, Mr Mayor,' replied Peter proudly. 'When I'm at an inn, and when I throw it down, it pays for all that I've had.'

The Mayor was interested. So interested, in fact, that he sat down at Peter's table. He was fascinated to hear that Peter had inherited this special kind of hat from his father, and that the hat had been of great help to Peter in the past.

'Oh yes,' related Peter, 'I would have starved without it many a time! Whenever I go to an inn, I take this hat with me. I eat and drink with my friends. And when it comes to paying the bill, I merely throw my hat down and, hey-presto! the bill is settled!'

The Mayor was so taken in that he was determined to buy this very special hat from Peter. He offered a hundred florins, and when Peter protested in the sacred name of his dead father, the Mayor offered another fifty. As Peter showed no intention of parting with his hat, the Mayor insisted on two hundred florins, and when Peter appeared to hesitate for a while, the Mayor clinched the deal with three hundred.

He was overjoyed. He counted out the three hundred florins, grabbed the greasy hat and ran out of the inn. On his way home, he called on all his friends and invited them to a special dinner at the most expensive place in town.

When his guests assembled — a good hundred of them — the Mayor placed the greasy hat carefully on his bald head and announced:

'We are ready. Let's go!'

The guests followed him, but that greasy, crumpled hat amused them so much that they couldn't help laughing and giggling.

'You won't laugh,' said the Mayor proudly, 'when you know what this hat can do! My word, you won't!' The guests were filled with curiosity, but the Mayor would not enlighten them. 'You'll see!' he boasted.

So they arrived at the inn. It was so expensive that each dish came at the price of two. The Mayor urged his guests to eat and drink regardless of cost, to treat themselves royally. The guests readily accepted his advice and began to eat. They ate so well that the larder was soon empty. Then they began to drink. They drank so well that soon the cellar was empty, too. Having emptied both the larder and the cellar, they were well content to go home.

It was time for the bill. The landlord spent a long time adding it all up and finally he presented it to the Mayor.

Whereupon the Mayor took the greasy hat off his head and winked at his guests.

'Now then, my friends,' he said, 'you will see what this hat can do!' Saying which, he threw it down so vigorously that it raised the dust.

'Well, landlord!' he demanded triumphantly. 'Is the bill settled to your satisfaction?'

The landlord smiled broadly and shook his head. No, it was not settled, how could it have been?

Perhaps, thought the Mayor, he didn't throw the hat down in the proper way. So he picked it up and threw it down again.

'Well, landlord, it is settled now, isn't it?'

The landlord smiled even more broadly and shook his head even more vigorously.

The Mayor snatched up the hat and threw it down again so forcefully that it nearly fell apart. 'Surely, landlord, you can't say that the bill isn't settled *now*, can you?'

'I can indeed,' replied the landlord gravely. 'You have not paid a single florin so far, and the bill comes to five hundred!'

It was then that the Mayor realized the truth: that wretched Peter Cheater had hoaxed him again! The Mayor paid the bill and ran all the way back to the Town Hall. He commanded two soldiers to come with him to get Peter, and hurl him into the clink. That would teach him a lesson, the rascally blackguard!

Peter saw them coming. He was cooking a potful of stew on the fire just then. Quickly, he grabbed the pot with the boiling stew, rushed to his front door, placed the pot on a tree-stump, sat in front of it and continued stirring the steaming stew with his ladle.

The Mayor arrived – and was so astounded that his mouth fell open. Of course he was astounded. There was

Peter, cooking a stew that was boiling and steaming on a tree-stump, without a fire underneath! The Mayor promptly forgot all about the horse and the hat, and enquired how Peter could possibly have achieved such a miracle?

'What miracle, Mr Mayor?' asked Peter

'Why, that you manage to cook a stew without a fire?'

'Oh that,' replied Peter modestly. 'You see, sir, this pot is three hundred years old. So many stews have been cooked in it during that time that it has got quite used to it, and it can now do it without a fire.'

'What a remarkable pot!' said the Mayor, in admiration.

'It certainly is,' replied Peter Cheater proudly. 'I've had many pots in my time, but they were ordinary ones. They didn't give two hoots whether I threw meat or onions into them. Every time I did, I had to light a fire under them first. But this one Mr Mayor, this one begins to warm up as soon as it sees the first piece of meat! So you can imagine that I wouldn't part with it for all the money in the world!'

The Mayor broke into tears. Upon Peter's sympathetic enquiry, he said, choking:

'I weep to hear that you won't part with it! Because I was about to offer you a hundred florins for it!'

Instead of replying, Peter took a ladleful of stew and held it under the Mayor's nose.

'Taste it, sir!' he urged.

The Mayor tasted it. He smacked his lips. It was good. Very good indeed.

'Now you see, Mr Mayor, the kind of stew my pot can cook. I can honestly tell you that if somebody offered me three hundred florins for it, I would still hesitate.'

'I am that somebody!' said the Mayor eagerly. 'I'll give you three hundred!'

Peter appeared to hesitate. Then he announced:

'It is lucky, Mr Mayor, that you are Mr Mayor. If you weren't Mr Mayor, I would not sell my pot for four hundred florins. But since you are Mr Mayor, I will sell it to you for three.'

The Mayor was most grateful. He would never forget Peter's kindness and generosity. He paid out the three hundred florins, took the pot and hurried home.

He went straight to the kitchen and placed the pot on the floor. Thereupon he ordered his servants to start peeling potatoes, cutting up meat and slicing onions so as to cook him a stew.

'On the floor?' asked the cook.

'Why, certainly on the floor!' he said. The servants stopped peeling and slicing and looked askance. The Mayor laughed.

'Do you take me for a fool? You are the fools if you can't see that this is a miraculous pot which cooks without fire! Just wait and see!'

The servants waited. But they saw nothing. The pot was full, but it wasn't cooking.

'Perhaps,' hesitated the Mayor, 'perhaps there isn't enough draught. We must blow!'

So he squatted down and the servants squatted down too. They blew. But the pot didn't warm up.

The Mayor sat on his haunches and groaned. He had been cheated again! Peter Cheater, the blackguard!

He jumped to his feet and shot out of the kitchen, straight back to Peter's house.

'How pleasant to see you again, Mr Mayor!' said Peter, welcomingly.

'Pleasant, is it?' fulminated the Mayor. 'We'll see if it's pleasant when you are in irons, in the clink, under lock and key, for the rest of your miserable life!'

Peter looked at the Mayor in mild surprise. 'What could have happened?' he enquired. 'It's not an hour since we parted in the greatest of good friendship.'

The Mayor enlightened Peter. How he was cheated and swindled! What a fake that pot was! How it refused to warm up, let alone cook by itself! What a blackguard Peter was!

'But of course!' laughed Peter. 'Of course the poor pot didn't cook!' He pointed to the tree-stump. 'You forgot to take the stump with you! I was about to bring it along to make sure that you would not be disappointed!'

The Mayor calmed down immediately. He was amazed. So that was it! He should obviously have had the stump as well! He reached for his purse.

'The tree-stump is worth nothing by itself,' said Peter generously, 'but to give you the pleasure, Mr Mayor, you may have it for a hundred florins.'

Having payed the money with alacrity, the Mayor shouldered the huge stump and staggered home with it. He hardly noticed the people in the town laughing at such an undignified sight. He was eager to get back into his kitchen to put the pot on the stump and watch it cooking. When he did so, however, the pot remained cold. No steam. Nothing.

The Mayor was so infuriated this time that he remained silent. All he did was to grind his teeth. But he ground them so loudly that the whole town heard it. And Peter heard it too.

Now Peter Cheater had a young sister called Esther Cheater. He called her in and handed her a tin whistle, explaining exactly what she must do. Then he took a hat (which had belonged to his great-grandfather and had seven impenetrable and uncrushable linings) put it on his head and went outside. He sat down by his front door to await the Mayor.

He hadn't long to wait. The Mayor appeared and stood silently in front of him. Except that he was still grinding his teeth. Peter remained silent, too, except that he nodded his head each time the Mayor ground his teeth.

'You are quite right, Mr Mayor,' he said. 'What you think is perfectly true.'

'How do you know what I am thinking?' ground out the Mayor.

'You are thinking, sir, that I am the biggest blackguard in the world.'

The Mayor was impressed by this discernment. 'And how did you know that?' he enquired.

'Chiefly because I, too, think that I am the biggest blackguard in the world.'

'And what else do you think I am thinking?' pursued the Mayor.

'That this time you will not have mercy on me.'

The Mayor was even more impressed. 'You are very quick-witted,' he acknowledged.

'Even quicker than that!' replied Peter Cheater, and produced a sizable bludgeon. He pressed it into the Mayor's hands and requested to be hit over the head with it. He knew, of course, that his hat with the seven linings would protect him well enough against any bludgeoning. The Mayor needed no prompting. He swung the bludgeon round and thump! he hit Peter over the head with it. Peter pretended to pass out and sank to the ground like a sack of potatoes.

At that very moment Esther Cheater came out of the house and blew her tin whistle three times. At the third blow Peter sprang to his feet and rubbed his eyes. 'That was a good sleep, that was!' he said, stretching. To which Esther replied:

'You would have slept 'til Doomsday if this whistle hadn't woken you up!'

This was too much for the Mayor. He wanted that whistle. He wanted it so much that he began to tremble. He must buy that whistle, he said. He always wanted a whistle like that! Peter said that he couldn't sell it. It was an heirloom. He couldn't part with it. But the Mayor was adamant. At length they struck a bargain. For a thousand florins and a pair of saddle-horses the tin whistle would be his. The Mayor ran straight back home to fetch the money and the horses.

'Well, my dear,' said Peter to Esther, 'it's time we went. Go in and pack.'

Esther went in and she had packed up everything by the time the Mayor returned with the thousand florins and the two saddle-horses. Peter pocketed the money, took the reins in his hand and gave the tin whistle to the Mayor.

'To make quite sure,' said Peter, 'that I am not cheating you this time, sir, I suggest that we try it out first.'

'Very well,' said the Mayor, 'but how?'

'I suggest, Mr Mayor, that I hit you over the head with the bludgeon, and that my sister blows the whistle. If you, Mr Mayor, don't revive then it is clear that I've cheated you, and I will return all the money. But if you do revive, then all is well!'

The Mayor thought this was an excellent suggestion. Accordingly, Peter hit him over the head thump! and the Mayor sank to the ground like a sack of potatoes. By the time he came round, Peter Cheater was miles away!

The Magic Doctor

ONCE upon a time there was a simple bootmaker. He was well known for his poverty, but he was even better known for the strong and beautiful boots and shoes he made.

One day his wife became ill: she complained of a terrible headache. The bootmaker plied her with all sorts of potions which the villagers suggested, but to no avail. She was still in pain and it didn't get better. The poor bootmaker racked his brains but still didn't know what to do. In those days there were no doctors in the villages. The bootmaker heard a rumour that there might be one in town and, what was more, a doctor who it was said could cure just about anything.

So he went to town and found the doctor's house. There were many people waiting but at last it was his turn to go in. The bootmaker forgot to remove his hat, but in the crowded waiting-room a man standing by the door accidentally knocked it off. The bootmaker took this to be the custom of the town, and went in.

The doctor sitting behind the table was no ordinary doctor: he was a magic doctor. He wore a black cloak and a tall pointed hat with a feather in it.

'What's wrong with you, then?' he asked.

The bootmaker shook his head – there was nothing wrong with him.

'So you are healthy?' enquired the doctor.

'I am,' said the bootmaker.

'Then perhaps you want me to make you ill?' joked the doctor.

The simple bootmaker tried to explain:

'No sir, but my wife is ill, and I wish to ask you to cure her.'

'Then why didn't she come herself?' demanded the doctor.

'Because she can't walk, so I came instead, because I can! So please give me a prescription.'

But the doctor refused to give him a prescription because, he said, patients must come to see him in person. So he sent the bootmaker away.

As he went out, the bootmaker took a good look round, to see what was involved in being a magic doctor. There was the cloak and the pointed hat, there were the tables and chairs, the papers and books, and there was the man at the door to knock people's hats off. It was quite a simple matter really, he thought.

Just then another patient came out holding his prescription.

'Excuse me, friend,' said the simple bootmaker pointing to the paper, 'how much did he charge you for that?'

'One gold piece,' said the other.

'Will you sell it to me?'

'No, I can't do that,' replied the man.

'Then please show it to me.'

Now the simple bootmaker was a very fine bootmaker, but he could neither read nor write. So he found a scrap of paper and copied out the odd marks he saw on the prescription, as best he could.

He took it to the chemist. The chemist was, of course, quite unable to make head or tail of it, but he kept a bottle of vinegar-and-water for use when presented with such illegible prescriptions.

When he got home, the bootmaker gave some of this medicine to his wife. She got better immediately, and by next morning she was completely cured.

'You see,' said the bootmaker to his wife, 'what good medicine that was! Did you know that it costs a gold piece to get a prescription? I took a good look round to find out what all this doctoring was about. As we have no doctor here in the village I have decided to become a magic doctor myself! It is a simple matter, really, and it pays better than bootmaking any day!'

His wife shook her head so much that it nearly fell off.

'You are only an ignorant peasant,' she told him, 'and you can't even read or write. How could you hope to learn all the things that doctors must know?'

'I am a good craftsman,' he replied, 'and doctoring is just another craft. I've seen how it is done, and what I've seen I have already learnt.'

'But you also need money to set up as a doctor,' objected his wife.

'There will be some money,' promised the bootmaker.

Saying which, he settled himself in front of his last and began to work. He worked with all his skill and with the utmost diligence. When he had finished, he had a pair of boots the like of which had never been seen before. He placed them in his satchel and set out to see the King. He planned to present the boots to the King and hoped that in return the King would reward him with a present of his own.

The royal sentry barred him at the gates of the palace. When the bootmaker told him why he had come, the sentry replied:

'I will only let you in if you promise to give me half the King's reward.'

The poor bootmaker had no choice but to agree. Then the royal steward barred him at the King's door. The bootmaker again explained why he had come and the steward said:

'I will only let you in if you promise to give me half the King's reward.'

The bootmaker had no choice yet again and promised to give the other half of the king's reward to the steward. So the door was opened to him and he stood in front of the King.

'What do you want, my man?' asked the King.

The bootmaker produced the pair of boots.

'Your Majesty, I made these boots and I would like to give them to you as a present.'

The King took them and tried them on. They fitted

perfectly. He was delighted with the splendid pair of boots, the like of which he had never seen before.

'You must have a reward for these,' said the King. 'I will measure out a plateful of gold for you.'

But the poor bootmaker shook his head. No, he had no wish for a plateful of gold.

'Well,' said the King, 'what can I give you instead?'

'Your Majesty,' replied the bootmaker, 'if you have no objection, would you kindly measure out a hundred strokes of the birch?'

The King was surprised, but he said, 'If that is what you want, you shall have it.' He called for three servants: one to hold the bootmaker, the other to wield the birch and the third to count the strokes.

The king gave the order and the first servant grabbed the bootmaker. Just as the second servant lifted his birch to begin the beating, the bootmaker said:

'Your Majesty, I promised the first half of my reward to the sentry. Would you please send for him?'

In came the sentry. 'Do you want half the reward?' asked the bootmaker.

'Not 'arf!' replied the sentry.

'Then give it to him!' laughed the king, and the servants grabbed the sentry. They gave him the full measure of fifty strokes.

Then it was the turn of the bootmaker again, but he told the king that the second half of the reward was promised to the steward. In came the steward and the fifty strokes were duly measured out on his back too.

The king was so amused by the bootmaker's cunning that he gave him two platefuls of gold.

The bootmaker went home. He had money now and set about to become a magic doctor. He rented a house, and he bought a black cloak and a pointed hat with a

feather in it; he bought tables, chairs, papers and books. He nailed a notice on the door saying that the magic doctor lived here, and he hired a man to stand at the door and knock people's hats off.

Next day the patients arrived. The bootmaker saw them in turn, and to each he gave a prescription at one gold piece a time. On these he drew the same odd marks which he had copied for his wife's prescription, and the patients took them to the chemist.

The chemist was of course quite unable to make head or tail of them, but he didn't want to send the patients back to the doctor. Instead he asked what was wrong with them, and measured out the proper medicine as best he could.

The bootmaker was lucky, because each patient was

given the correct medicine by the chemist, and the correct medicine cured every patient. So he became famous and patients came to him from far and wide.

At that time a certain Count lived near the village who was very fond of his horses. One night two of his finest were stolen by thieves. The Count searched everywhere, but in vain. So he called his coachman and told him, angrily, that if the horses were not found within three days, that would be the end of him.

The poor coachman set out to search for the stolen horses. For two days and nights he searched up hill and down dale. By the third day he was too tired to wander around the fields and woods, so he went to the village instead. When he saw the magic doctor's notice on the door, he thought that maybe the doctor would know

where the stolen horses were, and went in. He was so
sleepy while he waited along with the other patients that
he nearly dropped off, but when it was his turn to go in,
the man at the door gave him such a knock on the head that
he woke up.

The bootmaker-turned-doctor gave him the usual prescription and the coachman took it to the chemist. The
chemist perceived how sleepy the poor coachman was, but
of course he didn't know why. So he gave the coachman a
bottle of wake-up medicine, and the coachman drank some
of it straight away.

He was still very sleepy and would have been ashamed to
drop off in the middle of the village. So he walked down
the road and found a quiet spot just outside, where he
could lie down. It was night, and he tried to sleep. But by
now the wake-up medicine had taken its effect. It also
made his hearing much sharper and when he heard some
distant neighing he instantly recognized it to be that of the
stolen horses! He neighed back, and the horses answered
because they recognized his voice too.

The coachman took a little more of the wake-up
medicine. This had the effect of making his sense of smell
much sharper too, and thus in the darkness he managed
to smell his way to the horses. He had found them at last!

The Count was delighted to have his favourite horses
back safe and sound. The coachman told him all that had
happened, and how the prescription of the famous magic
doctor had led him to find the horses.

The Count told him to get the coach ready instantly,
because they were off to fetch the doctor and take him to
the King.

'Is His Majesty ill, then?' enquired the coachman.

'No, he isn't,' replied the Count, 'but there is trouble
sure enough. The Princess's diamond ring has been stolen,

and it must be found: and this doctor will surely be the man to find it!'

The Count went straight into the bootmaker's house.

'Are you the famous magic doctor?' he enquired.

The bootmaker realized that he was dealing with a Count and that discretion was the better part of valour.

'I am just an ordinary doctor,' he replied modestly.

'There is no need to be modest,' said the Count, 'because I know that you found my horses and that with your magic you know everything. So, I am sure you will know who stole the Princess's diamond ring. If you know who stole it, then I am sure you will know where it is. Then if you say where it is, I am sure it will be found. And if it is found, I am sure that His Majesty will reward you. And I am sure that His Majesty will reward me also for bringing you to him. So everybody will benefit: the King, the Princess, you and me.'

The bootmaker was worried. He had been lucky so far, but his luck couldn't hold out for ever. The King would find out that he was no magic doctor but just a bootmaker. Yet he had no choice but to go with the Count. So they drove straight up to the royal palace.

They were received with music and flowers, as befits the arrival of a famous magic doctor. The King immediately rewarded the Count for bringing the doctor to court, and then he addressed the bootmaker, without, however, recognizing him in his black cloak and pointed hat.

'I have need of your great knowledge, magic doctor. If my daughter's diamond ring is not found before her wedding, my people will blame me for the loss. They will say that I am no good as a King if I can't even defend my own daughter's property. So, magic doctor, go and find that ring for me. If you do you will be amply rewarded; if you do not, then I fear that you will be one head shorter.'

The poor bootmaker was in trouble. He knew well enough that he would not be able to find the ring and that he must therefore die. At any rate he would spend his last days in comfort, so he spoke to the King:

'I will do my best to find the ring, Your Majesty. All I would ask for is a private room in the palace, plenty of food and drink, and three servants.'

The King made all these provisions willingly, provided that the ring was found within three days.

The poor bootmaker went to his room. For the next two days he did precious little. He ate and he drank, and then he ate and he drank again. Occasionally he ate first and drank afterwards, and then he would drink first and eat afterwards. When he got bored with this, he started all over again. He lived like a King, but he still felt miserable.

On the third day – which he thought would be his last – he asked for his wife to be brought to him, because he wanted her to be at his side. But he told the King that in this important work two heads were better than one.

When she arrived, the bootmaker didn't worry her with his trouble. Instead, he boasted to her about his luxurious life, in that handsome room, with all the food and drink and with no less than three servants at his command! They talked until it was lunchtime, when the first servant brought in the first course.

The bootmaker pointed proudly at the servant and said to his wife:

'Look, he is the first!'

Hearing this, the servant was so alarmed that he nearly dropped his tray. The fact was that the Princess's diamond ring had been stolen by these very servants who now served the bootmaker! And they knew all about the famous magic doctor's knowledge and power. The servant steadied his tray, but he could hardly reach the door because his knees were knocking against each other so frightfully.

When they saw him in the kitchen, the other two servants knew that something was wrong. But they had no time to ask what it was because the second servant had to take in the roast turkey. As he brought it in, the boot-maker pointed at the servant and said to his wife:

'See him, he is the second of them!'

Hearing this, the servant was terrified. His teeth began to chatter so fast that he nearly bit his tongue in two. He could hardly grope his way back to the kitchen. When he finally got there, the three thieving servants were convinced that the magic doctor knew all about their crime. So they quickly resolved to hand the ring over to him and beg him not to tell the King of their wicked crime!

The third servant was in a terrible state when he brought in the pudding. He was shaking like a jelly he was so frightened. In fact, he was practically on his knees as he reached the table.

The bootmaker pointed at him and said to his wife:

'Mark him well. He is the third!'

Hearing this, the servant promptly dropped the tray. There was pudding all over the carpet, and he fell into it as he tried to retrieve the diamond ring from his pocket.

'What's the matter with you?' asked the bootmaker. 'Don't worry if the pudding is spoiled, you can bring another one.'

'It's not the pudding that is worrying me, kind sir, but the diamond ring which we stole from the Princess,' he said, as he held it out with trembling fingers.

The bootmaker was delighted at this unexpected turn of fortune. He was saved!

The servant was still on his knees, begging for mercy,

entreating the bootmaker to keep their secret from the King.

'I shall think of something,' replied the bootmaker, and began to pace up and down, thinking hard. He always did his best thinking on a full stomach and he was still savouring that excellent roast turkey. . . .

'A turkey!' he shouted. 'That's it, a turkey! Fetch me a turkey!'

The servant picked himself up. In all his life he had never heard of a turkey that could save three thieves from a King's wrath. But he dashed out and in no time at all the three servants brought in a big turkey which started to strut about the room.

'Now then,' ordered the bootmaker, 'hold that turkey and open his beak.'

He took the diamond ring and popped it into the

turkey's mouth — who was so surprised that he promptly swallowed it. 'Now let's wait until tomorrow,' said the bootmaker.

A band was playing early next morning, announcing the arrival of the King. He told the bootmaker that the three days were up and that there would be no more food or drink for him.

'And if you do not produce the ring today,' he added darkly, 'there won't be any life for you, either.'

'Your Majesty,' replied the bootmaker, 'the ring will be found today, but I require Your Majesty's help.' And he asked for the entire household of the palace to be summoned to the courtyard.

Trumpets were sounded, bells rung, and soon all the nobility — princes and dukes, earls and counts — assembled in the yard with their wives and children, and stood in a row. The bootmaker walked solemnly up and down, looking at each in turn. Then he shook his head.

'There is no ring here,' he announced. 'Please call for the staff.'

The trumpets sounded again, and all the servants and grooms and sentries of the palace trooped in, and stood in a row. The bootmaker proceeded with his solemn inspection, and finally shook his head again.

Then he asked for all the cattle and other animals to be brought in — all the horses, mules, donkeys, pigs and goats. There was hardly any room left in the courtyard and the nobility had to take refuge on the roof. The King, because of his rank, stood on the chimney. He was also getting rather impatient.

'No ring here, either,' announced the bootmaker, 'but if Your Majesty permits, I shall call in the poultry.'

The King gave a signal and there was a great sound of crowing and gobbling and quacking and gaggling, as the poultry was paraded in front of the bootmaker. He strutted importantly among the cocks and hens and geese and ducks, examining them all. And when he reached the turkeys, he took a sharp look and stopped suddenly. He shot out an accusing finger at the big turkey and shouted:

'There's your thief!'

The cook was then summoned and in no time at all, sure enough, the Princess's diamond ring was retrieved.

She was so delighted that she kissed the bootmaker on both cheeks. The King was so delighted that he gave the bootmaker a coach-and-four as a reward. The people were so delighted that they bestrew the road with flowers as the bootmaker and his wife drove home in their bright new coach.

'This is the end of the magic doctor,' said the boot-maker to his wife when they got home. 'We were lucky this time, but I shall not go on deceiving people any more. Let us sell the house and return to our peaceful old cottage.'

And that is exactly what they did. The magic doctor became a simple bootmaker once more. He made the most beautiful boots again, and he is making them still, to this day.

The Devil of a Bailiff

ONCE upon a time there was a farmer. He was very rich and very fat. He lived in a big house with his wife who was also very rich and very fat. He employed a lot of casual labourers on his farm, but he harassed and tormented them so much that none of them ever returned a second time. He was a cruel, selfish and mean employer.

He had a bailiff who looked after the farm for him and it was he who would engage the labourers for the farm.

Because the fat farmer had such a bad reputation locally, the bailiff had to go far afield to find such willing labourers as had not yet heard about this farmer, but by and large, things were running reasonably well.

Matters came to a head, however, one day when the bailiff himself gave notice. He refused to work for such a cruel farmer any more. He packed his bags and left without another word.

The fat farmer was now in real trouble. Without a bailiff, he told his fat wife, how could he hire labourers? Without labourers, who would cultivate the land? And without the land being cultivated, what would they eat in order to nourish their renowned fatness?

They considered the problem from every angle, but it never occurred to them to do the work themselves! They loved to eat, but they hated work.

So, one day, the farmer drove to town in the hope that he might find somebody there whom he could persuade to become his bailiff. But every man he approached inevitably asked the same question:

'Aren't you the famous fat farmer to whom no labourer will ever return for a second year?'

And the fat farmer had to admit that he was.

Whereupon the answer was invariably the same:

'I would rather work for the hangman!'

The fat farmer was in despair. When he got home he was so exasperated that he lost his temper. He threw down his hat and exclaimed:

'I've had enough! I would engage the devil himself for a bailiff if I could!'

No sooner were these words out of his mouth but that flames started flaring up in the stove. There was such a stinging cloud of smoke billowing out of it that the farmer had to rub his eyes. When he opened them again, he saw a short, dark figure standing in front of him. The fat farmer was so startled that he nearly fell off his chair.

'Who on earth are you?' he cried in alarm.

'I am the devil,' replied the other.

'And what do you want here?' bellowed the farmer.

'To become your bailiff,' said the devil.

'My bailiff?' fulminated the fat farmer. 'What do you mean?'

'Well, didn't you say just now that you would engage the devil himself for a bailiff, if you could?'

The fat farmer had to admit that he had. He calmed down a bit and agreed that he would engage the devil to become his bailiff. But first he enquired:

'Do you know anything about farming?'

The devil replied that of course he knew about it because he farmed in hell himself. There remained the question of wages, but the devil was very modest:

'For wages, I shall only take what your labourers are willing to offer me.'

'But I have no labourers at all!' complained the fat farmer.

'No matter, I'll do as I said. And, as for labourers, I shall look after that myself.'

And so it was agreed.

The devil took the cart next morning and by midday he returned bringing some labourers with him. He assigned them to their various tasks and he went around as and where his help was required. And so the work proceeded until the fat farmer came out, puffing and blowing. He stood for a while watching the labourers at their work, but then he grasped his stick and began to thrash those who happened to be nearest to him.

Quick as lightning, however, the devil bailiff appeared and stood in front of him.

'Put down that stick or you will be sorry,' he warned the fat farmer.

'What's that?' bellowed the fat man. 'How dare you give me orders, you dirty, miserable, filthy devil? I am master here and I beat whom I please! It's your turn now, just to show you who's who!'

With that, he raised his stick and was about to strike when the devil bailiff took a deep breath. So deep that he instantly became seven feet tall.

The fat farmer was so alarmed by the sudden growth of his bailiff that he promptly ran away. He didn't stop running until he got home and sat cowering by his fat wife. And there he remained until pay-day.

Then he came out at last, in order to measure out the dues to the labourers himself: so much wheat, so much barley, so much maize to each, whatever was owing to them. Except that he gave short measure to everyone, according to his fancy.

The devil noticed this and warned the fat farmer to give full measure to each man, otherwise, there would be trouble.

'What's that?' bellowed the farmer. 'How dare you give me orders, you dirty, miserable, filthy devil? You are dismissed here and now! You can go!'

The devil bailiff took another deep breath. So deep that he became nine feet tall.

The fat farmer quaked in his shoes. He was so alarmed that he proceeded to pay the wages in full, each according to his due. Then, very quietly, he returned to his house and sat cowering again by his fat wife. He didn't move from there, either, until one day the devil bailiff knocked on the door.

'What do you want?' asked the fat farmer.

'My year is up,' the devil said, 'and I will not stay any

longer. The farm is flourishing, and we have had twice as much harvest as last year. Let us go now and see what your labourers are willing to offer me.'

'What will they offer you?' laughed the fat farmer. 'Why, they can offer only what they have. And they have nothing! Ha-ha-ha!'

'We shall see,' said the devil.

The fat farmer was still laughing as they walked down into the village where his labourers lived. As they walked along the street, they happened to hear a young man and his bride quarrelling. The bride wanted him to escort her to the next village. The young man objected because he wanted to feed the animals first. At that the bride exclaimed:

'If you don't come with me, the devil take you!'

At which the fat farmer exclaimed:

'Did you hear that, bailiff? You can take the young man, he's been offered to you!'

'True,' said the devil, 'but not willingly. It is most unlikely that a bride should want to give up her young man to the devil.'

'You don't know these people,' said the farmer. 'If she sent her man to the devil, she meant it.'

'Very well,' replied the devil, 'let's put it to the test.'

With that he skipped across and, taking the young man by the neck, he spoke to the bride.

'Thank you for your present. We need young men just like this in hell.'

The bride was flabbergasted and began to weep and beseech the devil with all her heart that of course she wasn't serious and if he must take anybody at all, it should be herself, so long as he had mercy on her young man.

The devil released the man. The fat farmer and the devil continued up the village street until, once more, they

happened to overhear a quarrel. This time a married couple were having a row about their little boy who was standing between them, as to which of them should take him to school.

'Will you take him, or won't you?' asked the wife.

'No, I won't. You take him!' replied the husband.

'Well, if you won't, then the devil take him!'

The fat farmer burst into such laughter that his stomach was quaking.

'There you are, bailiff, there's your pay! But don't be too clever this time, because you'll get nothing for your pains!'

'It is true,' replied the devil, 'that they offered me their son, but where is the mother who would willingly give up her child to the devil?'

'You don't know these people,' said the farmer. 'She may regret it later on, but take my word the woman is in earnest now.'

'Very well,' replied the devil, 'let's put it to the test.'

With that he skipped across to the boy and spoke to his mother:

'Thank you for your present. We need little boys just like this in hell.'

The woman was flabbergasted and began to weep and beseech the devil with all her heart that, of course, she wasn't serious and if he must take anybody at all, it should be herself so long as he had mercy on her little son.

The devil released the little boy. They continued their walk. The fat farmer was roaring with laughter all the while, his stomach quaking and heaving.

'Why are you laughing so?' asked the devil.

'I laugh,' said the farmer, convulsed, 'because we've nearly reached the end of the village and you still haven't had any wages! If we go on like this, you'll have worked for me a whole year for nothing! Ha-ha-ha-ha!'

'Just you wait,' warned the devil. 'He who laughs last laughs longest!'

They continued on their way. As they reached the last house, they saw a group of labourers standing behind the fence, talking to each other.

'I hear the bailiff is leaving,' said one.

'He is, indeed,' said another.

'What will happen to us now?' asked a third,

'The farmer will go on tormenting us, what else?' said a fourth.

'The devil take him if he does!' said the fifth.

The devil glanced at the fat farmer.

'Go on laughing,' he encouraged him, 'if you have a mind to!'

The farmer sobered up quickly and, shaking his head, said in an unctuous voice:

'No, these people weren't speaking seriously, either.'

'Very well,' replied the devil, 'let's put it to the test.'

He skipped to the fence and addressed the labourers:

'Thank you for your present. I shall take the farmer, provided that you give him to me willingly.'

'We give him willingly all right,' they replied, 'so willingly that you can have his fat wife too, if you can carry them both!'

'Yes, I can carry them easily,' replied the devil. 'We need fat people just like these in hell!'

And, without further ado, he popped the fat farmer into a sack. He returned to the big house and popped the fat wife in as well. He tied a rope round the sack, swung it over his shoulder and didn't stop going until he had reached the deepest regions of hell.

The fat farmer and his wife are there to this day. If you don't believe it, look for them in the big house. And if you can't find them there, seek them in the other place.

The Honest Thief

ONCE upon a time there was a poor woman. She had a son called Michael. This Michael was an honest, frank and upright young man. Moreover, he was capable, skilful and clever. So clever, in fact, that soon word had spread throughout the kingdom that Michael could do anything.

Now, at that time, the ruler of the kingdom was a bad and dishonest king. He was also mean and envious. So envious, in fact, that when the news of Michael's fame reached him, he feared that it would overshadow his own.

It filled him with jealous rage and he determined to put an end to Michael. So he sent for him.

'Well, my fine fellow,' he sneered, 'I have heard all about you! Let us see, now. If you are as clever as they say, are you perchance a clever thief as well?'

'Your Majesty,' replied honest Michael, 'I never stole in my life, nor do I want to start now.'

'Yo-ho-ho!' cried the King triumphantly, 'but now you must! And I shall put you to the test straight away. If you succeed, my treasure is yours — I stole it myself, anyway. But, if you fail the test, you will go to the stake!'

The task that Michael had to perform was difficult. Twelve ploughmen were at work in the King's field, and Michael was commanded to steal their ploughs and oxen.

Honest Michael went home with a heavy heart and told his mother what he had to do.

'You must put your thinking-cap on, my son!' she said.

He sat down to think, and he thought and pondered. Then, after a while, he got up with a smile.

'Mother,' he said, 'may I please borrow your cockerel and the twelve black hens?'

His mother was puzzled but she gave her permission. Michael took the hens and the cockerel to the King's forest, by the edge of which the twelve ploughmen were hard a-ploughing in the King's field. Michael released the birds and gave a great shout:

'Halloooooo-halloooooo! There they go! The wildcock and his magic hens! Lucky he who catches them!'

The ploughmen promptly left their ploughs and ran to chase the hens. The hens took fright and plunged into the forest: the ploughmen followed after them.

Honest Michael, meanwhile, strolled across the field to gather up the ploughs and oxen, and drove them home. According to the King's stipulation they now belonged to him. He sent his mother with the message that the King must not expect to have his ploughs and oxen back again.

The King was very angry. Next day he sent for Michael:

'Well, my fine fellow,' he growled, 'I hear you managed to steal my ploughs and oxen.'

'I managed,' replied Michael, modestly.

'Very well, you were lucky this time, but now you must perform another task. My sacks of corn are kept in a barn under the constant guard of my soldiers. You must steal the corn by morning. If you succeed, my kingdom is yours — I stole it myself, anyway. But if you fail, yo-ho-ho! you go to the stake!'

'I shall do my best, Your Majesty,' replied Michael.

He thought and pondered again. How could he remove the sacks of corn from under the noses of those constantly vigilant soldiers?

The King, meanwhile, had a private word with them. He called them in and offered them some brandy. He told them to be especially on their guard that night. And should the cursed Michael come near the barn, the soldiers must beat him up mercilessly! They drank a toast to that.

But Michael had overheard this and promptly knew what to do. He made a man out of straw and dressed it in his own hat and coat. He placed it stealthily in front of the barn. Hiding himself — he sneezed a great sneeze!

The soldiers dashed out — rather the worse for drink by then. They heard the sneeze. They saw the straw man. They saw Michael's hat and coat. 'It's Michael,' they shouted! 'At him!' With the giddy fervour of the brandy they fell on the figure — they could have sworn it was Michael who had come to steal the corn! So, Bang! Wallop! Thump! What a thrashing they gave him! Dust and straw flew everywhere! Beat the rascal! You could hardly see the straw man — and the soldiers were so thorough that, sure enough, only the hat and coat remained.

A job well done, they thought, and staggered back to the King. No more fear of Michael, they boasted, he won't come to steal the corn from the barn again! He's been beaten to a pulp! The King was delighted with the news, made his soldiers rest and gave them another drink.

During which time, Michael stole quietly away with all the King's corn.

His mother again took his message to the King that the task had been accomplished.

The King looked black as thunder. He ran into the barn: there was not a single grain to be seen. So the King sent for Michael again. He was really furious this time.

'Well, my fine fellow,' he said between clenched teeth, 'you have stolen my corn, what?'

'Yes, Your Majesty.'

'Very well. But now we come to real business. My

golden stallion is in the stable, and my grooms guard him day and night. If you can steal him my crown is yours — I stole it myself, anyway. But if you fail, yo-ho-ho! you go to the stake!'

Michael thought and pondered once more. Then he had an idea. He dressed himself as a gipsy, slung a flagon of brandy over his shoulder and tucked his fiddle under his arm. Thus equipped, he went that night to the stable and knocked on the door.

Had the grooms known it was Michael they would have refused to let him in, because the King had made it their duty to mount special guard that night. But when they saw that it was merely a poor gipsy with a fiddle — and a flagon of brandy! — they opened the door. Michael sat down by the manger. He saw how well guarded the stallion was: one groom held him by the halter, another by the tail, and a third was astride on his back.

Michael told a few stories, and the grooms laughed. He offered his flagon of brandy, and the grooms drank. Then he produced his fiddle.

Now, if there was one thing Michael could do better than any other thing, it was to play the fiddle. So he struck up a gay tune, and the grooms danced. He played wild songs, and the grooms sang. He played sad laments, and the grooms wept. All the while they took sips of his brandy.

It was late into the night by then, so Michael played a soothing lullaby, and the grooms lay down and fell asleep.

Michael got up. He lifted the first groom gingerly off the back of the stallion and placed him astride the manger. He placed a twist of hemp in the hand of the second who held the stallion's tail, and left the third groom holding the halter but he unhitched the other end. So, leading the stallion out of the stable, Michael rode quietly home.

The King came striding confidently to the stable next morning. The stallion was gone! He was beside himself with fury. He thundered at the grooms:

'Where's my stallion, you rascals?'

The grooms woke with a start — still rather hazy from the brandy.

'But I am still sitting on him!' said the one sitting astride the manger.

'And I am still holding him by the halter!' said the other with the empty halter in his hand.

'And I am still holding him by the tail!' said the third with the twist of hemp.

The King swore at them until he was blue in the face. He resolved that, henceforth, he would guard his property himself, and that he would destroy Michael, come what may!

He brooded over the best way to catch Michael. 'Yo-ho-ho!' he gloated, 'I've got it!'

He sent for Michael at once.

'Well, my fine fellow,' he fumed, 'so you've got my stallion!'

'I have, Your Majesty,' replied Michael respectfully.

'Very well, then. Tomorrow I shall sit down to lunch. You must come and steal my lunch from me. If you succeed, my royal sword is yours — I stole it myself, anyway. But if you fail, yo-ho-ho! you go to the stake!'

Michael thought and pondered.

Next day the King and Queen sat down to lunch. The dish stood in front of them on the table. Suddenly, they saw a hand reaching for it through the window!

You must know that the night before Michael had carved a wooden hand and painted it. He tied it to a rope and secured the rope to the wishing-well in the King's garden. He was now hiding beneath the window and was

pushing the hand towards the dish when the King noticed
it. The King gave a triumphant yell:

'That's Michael! Yo-ho-ho! we shall catch him now!'

The King grabbed the hand. The Queen grabbed the
King. The maid grabbed the Queen. The cook grabbed
the maid. And they pulled. They pulled and pulled until
the rope gave way. The King, the Queen, the maid and the
cook fell flat on their backs in a heap. By the time they got
to their feet at last and looked round, Michael and the dish
had disappeared.

He and his mother had a good dinner that night.

When they had just finished and were about to sit back,
there was a loud knocking on their cottage door. The King
himself stood on the threshold, in a towering rage. He was
too impatient to wait for the morrow.

'I see you've had a good dinner!' he spluttered.

'Yes thank you, Your Majesty,' said Michael.

'Very well! This very night you have another test for
your ingenuity – the last one. If you succeed, my
daughter is yours! I did not steal her as it happens, but I
want her to marry a man who is worthier than myself.
Hence all these tests. But if you fail, yo-ho-ho! you will
certainly go to the stake!'

Michael's task was to steal the Queen's golden ring off her finger by morning.

Michael crept into the royal palace that night and hid outside the King's bedroom. He overheard the King speak to the Queen:

'I am just going out for a while to see if Michael's about. When I return, my dear, give me your ring. It will be safer on my finger!'

The King came out of the dark bedroom and shuffled down the corridor. Michael walked straight in. Now, if there was one thing Michael could do even better than play the fiddle, it was to change his voice. So he said, sounding exactly like the King:

'My dear, give me the ring quickly. That cursed Michael might come in at any moment!'

Without a word, the Queen gave him the ring. Michael hid behind the door, and when the King returned he slipped quietly away.

The King climbed into bed.

'My dear, give me the ring!' he said to the Queen.

'Do not be foolish, my love,' replied the Queen indignantly, 'you have already asked me for it just now and I have given it to you!'

The King stared. He opened his mouth. But he was speechless with impotent rage.

He was still speechless next day, when Honest Michael himself came to the palace.

'I have performed the tasks, Your Majesty,' he said, 'and I have come to claim the rewards you promised: your treasure, your kingdom, your crown, your royal sword and the Princess, your daughter!'

Great was the joy in the Kingdom when Honest Michael married the Princess, and great the happiness when he ruled for ever and a day.

The Mayor's Egg

ONCE upon a time there was a small parish. The gamekeeper of the parish was tramping across a meadow one day when he saw a prodigiously enormous pumpkin on the ground.

'Well, I never!' he exclaimed in amazement, 'what in the name of wonder is that?'

He'd seen some marrows in his time, long and striped or fat and smooth, but never before in his life had he seen such a huge round yellow thing as this.

He picked it up, felt it, smelt it, but he couldn't make head or tail of it. So he took it to the village hall, where the Parish Council happened to be in session. The gamekeeper placed the pumpkin on the council table. The wise Councillors looked at it and were equally flabbergasted. They stared at the pumpkin and they stared at each other.

Then the wisest and oldest of them all spoke up:

'I have had a very long life, but never in my born days have I seen the like of this before. What could it be?'

The second wisest and oldest Councillor took his turn:

'I, too, have been through a lot in my life, but this is beyond my experience.' And he cast an enquiring look at the third wisest and oldest Councillor.

'As to that,' said he, 'I have some experience of most things myself, but this object defeats me. Let us hear what our Mayor thinks, as he is the wisest of us all.'

The Mayor stood up and spoke solemnly:

'Honourable Councillors, I declare that this object – judging by its shape – is an egg.'

Wherewith the Councillors felt themselves instantly enlightened.

'Of course it's an egg! What else could it possibly be but an egg?'

The gamekeeper himself agreed, and remembered how warm the pumpkin had felt when he first picked it up in the meadow.

But the Mayor wasn't Mayor for nothing. He also wanted to know precisely what kind of egg this was.

'A dragon's egg!' exclaimed the oldest Councillor.

'A camel's!' announced another.

But the Mayor preferred to consult the gamekeeper. That worthy man recalled that when he first noticed the pumpkin he saw a strange, large, four-legged animal in the vicinity. It was running and it had a mane and a long hairy tail!

Now it so happened that at that time, in that small parish, horses were rarely if ever seen. The peasants only had oxen for their ploughs and carts. They even went to weddings by oxcart.

But the Mayor, who wasn't Mayor for nothing, had certainly seen horses and mares in his time.

'It is a mare's egg!' he cried triumphantly.

The Councillors were nonplussed. 'But how could that be?' asked one of them. 'Mayors do not lay eggs. With respect, Mr Mayor, even you cannot lay an egg.'

The Mayor looked pained. 'I know that,' he said impatiently. 'And I haven't got a long hairy tail either. No. I mean the egg of a mare. M.A.R.E. A horse of the female kind.'

The Councillors listened attentively and suddenly light dawned. Their faces lit up and they were delighted that the Mayor had solved the mystery.

'Naturally! That's it! Who else but a horse could have laid such a prodigiously enormous egg?'

'Fellow Councillors,' announced the Mayor, 'we have done well so far. The question now arises, however, as to what we should do with it?'

'Hatch it!' came the unanimous reply.

'Yes, indeed, but how? We have no horses.'

There was silence. Everybody pondered for a while. They thought and thought and racked their brains. But it was the Mayor, once more, who found the solution.

'I am of the opinion,' he said, 'that we should take this splendid egg and hatch it ourselves!'

There was again general agreement among the Councillors.

To set a good example, the Mayor took it upon himself

to sit on the egg first. He was followed by the others in turn, according to age and precedence. Each of them sat for a day. Exactly as broody hens do.

The Council would have continued to sit in turn on the pumpkin 'til Doomsday except for a rumour which emanated from the neighbouring village. It was said there that the worthy Councillors were sitting on an addled egg! It must have been addled because it hadn't hatched! Hearing this, the Councillors expostulated and refused to sit on the mare's egg any further.

The Mayor was deeply wounded. He could have sworn that the little foal was already moving inside the egg. He shook it. He smelt it. He required the Councillors to smell it themselves. But the Councillors refused to listen to him. According to them, the egg had a distinct smell. It was addled!

After a long discussion, however, it was decided that the addled egg should be taken to the parish border and placed on the top of the hill, whence it could be rolled down towards the very village which was so insolent in its disparagement of the Parish Council.

The whole parish came out to witness the occasion and to see that slanderous village next door get what it deserved.

The egg was brought forth. Certainly, it smelt to high heaven. The Mayor wheeled it up the hill in his barrow and, as everyone was holding his nose, he lifted it out and rolled it downhill all by himself. The egg rolled and rolled until, at the bottom of the hill, it rolled into a hawthorn bush. It must have hit a stone because it broke to smithereens. And at that very instant, a small rabbit sprang out of the bush and the whole parish broke into triumphant shouts:

'The foal! Look! There goes the little horse! After him!'

The entire population sprang up and began to run after the rabbit.

Only the Mayor remained standing on top of the hill, surrounded by his Councillors. Seeing that it was useless to run because he knew that nobody could catch up with the swift little creature, he drew himself up.

'Did I not tell you,' he sighed, 'that the foal was already moving? You should have been a little more patient.'

The Councillors stood around in silence and looked at him with a new respect. He certainly wasn't their Mayor for nothing!

King Greenbeard

B EYOND the seven kingdoms, and further still, where
the short-tailed piglets grub, there lived, once upon
a time, a greenbearded king.

This King Greenbeard took it upon himself one day to
go on a journey. He travelled far – he must have wandered
the length of a hundred needles at least – when one day he
realized that it must be fully seventeen years since he left
home. He had journeyed so far that he was exceedingly
tired and thirsty. So he sat down on the bank of a brook and
then lay flat on his stomach the better to take a good long

88

drink. Hardly had he gulped once or twice but somebody grabbed him by the beard. He tried to pull back, but couldn't. So he called into the brook:

'Do you hear me you I-don't-know-who, let go of my beard or else!'

But he was pulled even harder. He was pulled into the water so hard that he nearly drowned. Then from the water there came a voice.

'I will let go of your beard if you give me that of which you don't know in your own country.'

'What is there of which I don't know in my own country? I know every last pin in the place!' said King Greenbeard.

'Just promise that you will give me that of which you don't know there,' said the King of the Devils. Because it was he!

'Very well, then, it is yours. And much good it may do you!' said King Greenbeard. He was most uncomfortable, lying there on his stomach. At last, the King of the Devils released him. On the homeward journey the King wondered what there was in his country of which he didn't know.

On his arrival home a handsome young lad ran towards him and embraced him.

'My dearest father, you have been away for so long, but oh! it is good that you are back at last. I am John.'

The King stared. Then he pushed the boy away.

'Whose father am I? Whose son are you? I don't know you!'

But his wife explained to him that, sure enough, John was his son. He was born soon after the King had left home.

It was only then that the King realized what he had done! He had promised the King of the Devils that he

would give him that of which he did not know in his own
country. And it was to be his handsome young son! He
could have eaten himself. He thought for a moment that
he would not keep his promise, but then he realized that
the King of the Devils would come himself to fetch that
which was his.

The King called his son. He told him all. But the young
man was not afraid and reassured his father that it would be
best if he went. Next day he got ready and left home.

He went and wandered beyond the seven kingdoms
until he reached the brook where his father's beard had
been held. Seven golden ducklings were swimming across
the water and on the bank he saw a cloak flapping in the
breeze. He bent down to pick up the cloak to stuff it into
his satchel, when one of the seven golden ducklings turned
into a beautiful girl who said:

'Handsome prince, I know who you are and where you
are going. You are King Greenbeard's son and you are
going to my father, because he won you from yours. Give
me back the cloak and I will repay your kindness!'

The Prince gave it to her. The girl dressed herself and
pulling a golden ring off her finger she gave it to him.

'Guard this ring. You will be able to enter twelve castle
doors by merely turning it. Once you are inside the palace,
my father will set you such tasks that, even if you were an
angel, you would not be able to accomplish them. But I
shall help you. Around eight o'clock tonight I shall come
to your window in the shape of a bumble-bee. Let me in,
and you need not fear!'

The young Prince slipped the ring on his finger, took
his farewell and set out towards the King of the Devils'
palace. Twelve castle doors barred his way, but at a turn of
the ring they each opened. At last the palace door itself
opened, and there stood the King of the Devils.

'Your Majesty, here I am!'

'That is well,' replied the King. 'But you speak bravely – perhaps you don't know who I am?'

'I know well enough,' replied the Prince, 'you are no different from my father: he is a king, you are a king too, and that's all there is to it.'

The King became angry. 'How dare you treat me so lightly! You will have three tasks to perform. If you master them, well and good; if not, that will be the end of you! Here is a cabbage leaf, take it. I shall lock you in your room and if by morning you have not made a feathered hat out of it, you may start praying!'

The Prince was then locked into a room where food and drink was provided. When he was left alone, he began to groan:

'What a devil's spawn you are!' he said. 'I will never be able to perform this task as long as the world exists!'

He would have gone on groaning, had he not heard a buzzing by the window. Then he remembered the beautiful girl. He went to the window and heard the bumble-bee speak:

> '*Let me in, my prince so true!*
> *To render help I come to you!*'

He opened the window immediately. The bumble-bee flew in and turned into a beautiful girl.

'My sweet heart, my dearest love, tell me how I can help you?'

John told her that he must make a feathered hat out of a cabbage leaf, and that he was very frightened.

'If that's your trouble,' said the girl, 'then there's no trouble. Where is the cabbage leaf?'

'Here it is.'

'Just take a look!' And in that instant the most beautiful feathered hat lay on the table.

The Prince stared until his eyes nearly popped out. He had never seen such a thing before. Then the girl spoke:

'I shall come again tomorrow night, but don't keep me waiting as you did tonight. When you hear my buzz, let me in. I am going now, so open the window.'

Instantly she became a tiny little bumble-bee again, and flew away.

The Prince lay down, happy in the knowledge that the King of the Devils would have something to look at when he saw the hat. Early next morning the King came to the Prince. As soon as he opened the door, he saw the feathered hat on the table. He told the Prince:

'I must say you have performed this task most thoroughly!'

'I have indeed!' was the pert reply.

'Hm. Since you are so proud I'll give you a task which you certainly won't be able to perform!'

The King of the Devils went out and returned with a potful of cabbage water.

'Now, if you don't make me silver spurs out of this by morning, your life is at an end!'

The Prince merely shrugged his shoulders.

'They will be made, with God's help!'

So the King went out and left the Prince alone.

'Cabbage water and silver spurs! Nothing will come of this. What a crazy king to think of such things!' he thought.

He waited patiently until eight o'clock and, sure enough, the bumble-bee came again.

> *'Let me in, my prince so true!*
> *To render help I come to you!'*

He let her in, and again she changed into the beautiful girl he had seen on the bank of the brook. He told her what her father had demanded. Again it was as nothing to her. From the cabbage water she fashioned such a pair of silver spurs that they would have delighted the eyes of anyone. How happy was the Prince! He embraced and kissed the girl fervently. Then she shook herself, became a tiny bumble-bee again and flew away.

Next day the King of the Devils nearly fell over in amazement when he saw the lovely pair of silver spurs. But he had not had enough yet: he was after the Prince's life. He brought a jug of pure, strained water.

'Now, if you don't make me some brass scales out of this by morning, you might as well start writing your last will and testament!'

The Prince said nothing. He waited until the evening in the hope that as all had gone well so far, this final task might go well too. However, when the bumble-bee turned into the girl and she was told of the task, she shook her head saying that it was beyond her!

'But do not despair,' she said. 'We shall leave this place together because neither of us has a future here. I will touch you with my wand and turn you into a golden ring; I shall turn my chestnut mare into a golden apple and I shall become a bird.'

No sooner said than done. The Prince became a golden ring, the chestnut mare a golden apple, and the girl a bird: she took the ring in her beak and the apple in her claws and she flew away on the wind.

Next morning the King found neither the Prince nor the girl. He realized that they must have escaped together and he told his servant: 'Go after them and bring them back!'

How the servant ran! He ran like lightning.

And the bird told the ring:

'There is such a swift wind at my back, that I am sure they are pursuing us!' Presently she saw a dense bush and landed right in the centre of it, to hide.

The servant soon caught up with them and searched everywhere but found nobody. He went home and told the King:

'Your Majesty, I found nothing, not so much as the dirt under my nails. All I saw in the desert was a bush with a small bird in its middle.'

'That was it, you ass!' shouted the King. 'I see I've got to go myself, I can't trust anyone here!'

If ever there was speed, the king of the Devils was twice as fast. The little bird too was flying at her swiftest. She knew that if she did not reach the border of the Devil's kingdom soon, she would be caught. She could feel a mighty wind at her back. She could see the Devil behind her, like forked lightning. But just then, in the nick of time, she flew over the border and away to safety! The might of the king of the Devils did not reach beyond the border of his country and, when he saw that the little bird flew safely over it, he became so furious that he promptly exploded.

The little bird changed back into a beautiful girl, the golden ring into a prince and the golden apple into a chestnut mare. They mounted the horse and rode into the country of King Greenbeard.

There followed a fine wedding, and a great feast. I was at the feast too, playing the fiddle, and I ate so many black puddings and sausages that I couldn't eat another morsel, not even the next day!

And the young couple lived happily ever after.

Almafi and the Flying Palace

ONCE upon a time, beyond the seven seas, there was a poor couple. They had no possessions, neither did they have any children.

But they did have an apple tree.

One fine autumn day the poor woman was standing under the tree when quite suddenly three apples dropped to the ground in front of her. They split open and behold! three lovely baby boys emerged from them!

The poor couple marvelled and rejoiced. The first thing they did was to name the children, and they both agreed that each of the boys would be called Almafi: which means, son of the apple. They would be called First Almafi, Second Almafi and Third Almafi.

The children grew and flourished. They looked so alike that no one except their parents knew them apart.

When the boys had reached their eighteenth year, their father spoke to First Almafi:

'My son, you see how poor we are. It is time that you went out to seek your fortune.' His mother baked him a barley loaf, and he took his farewell.

He journeyed all day, and by nightfall he was tired and hungry. He sat down by the roadside and pulled the barley loaf out of his satchel. He had hardly taken a few mouthfuls before he saw a white-haired old man standing in front of him.

'Good evening, my son!' greeted the old man.

'It is indeed good, father!' said the boy.

'Yes, my son, I can see that it is for you because you have something to eat. But I have not eaten for these last three days.'

'I have only this loaf; but what I have I will share with you,' said the boy.

The old man thanked him and, having eaten, spoke:

'I know that you are seeking your fortune, my son, and perhaps I can help you in return for your kindness. Stay here until night comes and watch for the rising of the scythe-star. Whichever way its shaft points, that will be the way for you to go. You will find your fortune in that direction! But mark: when you come to a swiftly-flowing stream, do not be afraid but step into its torrent bravely. It is an enchanted stream and will bear you as if it were a meadow!'

The boy listened attentively as the old man continued:

'In the centre of the stream you will find the most beautiful of all waterlilies. Do not be tempted to pick any

of them, for if you do you will be lost. Once you are safely
on the other side of the stream you will see a meadow where
every blade of grass and every rose is made of silver. You
will be enchanted: but do not be tempted to pick a single
blade of grass or rose, for if you do you will perish. Beyond
that meadow you will come to a field of gold, but again, do
not be tempted to pick a single golden blade of grass or
rose, for if you do you will suffer. But if you manage to get
across it, you will find your fortune on the other side!'

The boy thanked the white-haired old man, who, saying farewell, vanished into thin air.

First Almafi waited for the rising of the scythe-star and
set out in the direction of its shaft. He soon found the
swiftly-flowing stream, but its raging torrent threw up
such spume and spray that he doubted the old man's
assurances. But, he thought, what will be, will be. So he
stepped in and, sure enough, he managed to walk as if on
dry land. And there in the centre were the waterlilies, each
of them more enchanting than the next. He again remembered the old man's warning, and he again doubted
it. 'What harm,' thought he, 'could a beautiful lily do
to me?' So he picked one and placed it in his buttonhole.
But lo! he was instantly changed into a fish and vanished in
the spray.

Time passed, and there was no sign of First Almafi. So
the father spoke to Second Almafi:

'My son, go and seek your fortune, and search for your
brother.'

Second Almafi set out, and took the same road as his
elder brother had taken. He, too, had a barley loaf and he,
too, sat down by the roadside. The white-haired old man
appeared in front of him just as he had appeared to his
brother, and they shared the loaf exactly as his elder
brother had shared his. Second Almafi received the same

instructions from the old man. Having warned him about
the waterlilies, the old man added:

'Alas, your brother picked one of them and so he is
lost. Guard yourself, my son, lest the same fate befalls you
too!'

The old man said farewell and vanished into thin air.

Second Almafi reached the swiftly-flowing stream and
managed to cross it. He was sorely tempted to pick one of
the enchanting lilies and had already reached out to do so,
but, just in time, he remembered his brother's fate. When
he reached the silver meadow, however, he was quite
unable to restrain himself. And as he plucked a silver rose
and placed it in his buttonhole, he instantly turned into a
silver snake and slid behind some stones.

So now two Almafi brothers had disappeared.

It was the turn of Third Almafi to seek his fortune now.
He took his barley loaf and set out on the same road which
his brothers had taken. He met the same old man with the
white hair, and received the same instructions. The old
man added:

'I see you are of stout heart, my son, so perhaps you will be wiser than your two brothers!'

Almafi remembered the old man's warning as he crossed the stream and the silver meadow. But when he came to the golden meadow he found he could hardly restrain himself. He reached out for a rose and only just recalled in time the warning he had been given. So he crossed safely over the field of gold and found himself on the other side.

A vast and empty desert greeted him. Not a blade of grass, not a single tree — just a limitless stretch of sand.

'Did the old man deceive me after all?' he asked himself. 'Surely, I will perish in this emptiness!' But he continued on his way. His feet sank deep in the sand with every step he took and the sun beat mercilessly down on him. At night it was bitterly cold, but he marched on regardless. By the following day he was hungry, and by the third, he was so exhausted that he sank to the ground.

How long he lay there he knew not but he suddenly heard a tremendous humming in the air. He looked up into the copper-coloured sky to see what could be the cause of such a mighty rumbling roar. To his amazement, he saw a beautiful palace floating through the air!

And only when it was about to disappear did he catch sight of a lovely young maiden sitting on its balcony. In that single moment, he felt himself falling desperately in love with her. And he knew that so long as life remained, he would pursue that vision.

He got up and with renewed vigour continued his journey in the desert. By the next day, however, his gnawing hunger blurred his eyes and he rubbed them in disbelief when he thought that a bird had landed in front of him in the sand. Could it be a hen, an ordinary farmyard chicken? Could some mysterious agency be sending him something to eat?

The hen sat there, just waiting. Almafi could have reached out to devour it. But he felt sorry for the bird, especially as it seemed to be nearly as exhausted as himself.

'Come, little hen!' he said softly, 'I shall not hurt you. Let me carry you instead, so we may seek some refuge together.'

Instantly, the bird disappeared and, in its place, stood the white-haired old man!

'I came to test you once more, my son,' he said. 'Your pity overcame your greed and I shall grant you a wish in return.'

Almafi pondered for a moment. He could have asked for food; he could have asked the way to find the maiden in the flying palace. But, instead, he said:

'If it is in your power, Sir, release my two brothers from their enchantment and restore them to my parents.'

'You choose well,' replied the old man, 'and I grant your wish. Your brothers are already on their way home. And if you continue your journey bravely, you will find your fortune.'

Saying which, he disappeared into thin air.

Almafi continued for another day. He was near to collapsing again when, in the far distance ahead, he saw an enormous castle. He gathered all his remaining strength and made his way towards it. When he finally reached it, he was filled with wonder and surprise. There was not a single window in the whole of that edifice. Just a tiny door tucked away. 'No matter,' he thought. He opened it and found himself in a colossal and dazzling hall, filled with light, although there wasn't a single window. He saw a row of tables in front of him, and walked up to them.

On the first table there was a bowl of porridge and a tablet by its side with some writing on it. It said that this was the fairies' porridge and he who ate it would never be hungry again. The boy ate voraciously and, when he had finished all the porridge, he truly felt as if satisfied for all time.

He walked to the second table. There was a bottle with some liquid in it and a tablet which said that this was the fairies' drink and he who drank it would never be thirsty again. Almafi did not hesitate and drank the lot. He truly felt as if his thirst had been quenched for all time.

The third table had a small jar containing some ointment. The tablet by its side said that this was the fairies' ointment and he who anointed himself with it would obtain the strength of a thousand men. The boy took the jar and duly anointed himself.

So he came to the fourth table. It held a sword. This was the fairy-sword, said the tablet, and it was invincible. The boy took it and buckled it on his belt.

The fifth table had a small jug containing some oil. The tablet said that he who anointed his eyes with it should see everything, even into the depths of the earth and the waves. Without hesitation he dabbed it on his eyes.

And then he realized the value of what he had been given. The old man with the white hair had truly led him to a fortune.

He felt perfectly equipped now to continue his search for the maiden on the balcony of the flying palace. Having rested, he set out on his journey.

Almafi roamed the world for a full year, searching for his love. Through many dangers and adventures he had reason to be grateful to the fairy sword in his hand, and for the strength of a thousand men with which he vanquished his foes. He had no worries about food or drink — but he had an aching void in his heart. Come what may, he must find the flying palace!

One day, he came to the foot of an immense mountain,

with its peak in the clouds. Surely, he thought, he would be able to glimpse the flying palace from its summit!

It took him seven days to reach the top of the mountain. It was wreathed in swirling cloud as he looked all around. The power which the fairies had given his eyes made it possible for them to penetrate the dense ramparts of cloud and he saw a limitless horizon. And as he looked, he saw the flying palace far away, coming towards him!

The summit on which he stood was so high that the palace was at Almafi's own level as it came ever nearer. When it was almost within reach, Almafi leapt off the topmost rock and landed in the courtyard of the palace itself!

He got up and looked around. There was no one to be seen. So he made straight for a door and strode through innumerable apartments until he reached the balcony. There sat the young girl, weeping.

'My dearest heart,' asked Almafi, 'why do you weep?'

'Because,' sobbed the girl, 'I have been chained to this palace, this balcony, for the last three years!'

And indeed, Almafi saw, she was bound hand and foot by stout chains secured with massive locks. There was no need to search for a key. His strength was key enough, and in an instant the girl was free.

'Now tell me, my dearest heart, how came you to be in this accursed palace?'

The girl told her story thus:

'I am a princess. My father the King went out hunting one day, when he encountered a monster. He shot an arrow at it. The monster warned my father that he would pay dearly for wounding him, and that he would abduct his only daughter, no matter how well-guarded she might be. At first, my father dismissed this with a smile, knowing how secure his castle was, but day-by-day he became more anxious, although he never told us the cause of his worries. He kept the strictest watch over me and I was accompanied wherever I went. But later on he may have convinced himself that perhaps the monster had forgotten his threat, and relaxed his guard over me: be that as it may, I stole out one day to take a walk in the royal gardens, all by myself. Suddenly, I heard a tremendous humming in the air and saw a flying palace which seemed to make straight for me! It descended within a few feet of me and a monster leapt out and gathered me up in his arms. When I came to my senses again I found myself here on this balcony. I was not chained to begin with and was allowed to walk to my apartment in the palace, but the monster visited me daily and demanded that I become his wife. I would not listen to him and tried to escape, which is why he chained me to the balcony. Otherwise I am treated well, although he still comes to see me every day to see if I have changed my mind. But even if we fly around until Doomsday, I shall never become his wife!'

'Where can I find this monster?' asked Almafi, darkly.

'There are a hundred rooms in this palace and he lives in the hundredth. He is invincibly strong. He gets his strength from the wine of a barrel which is kept in the cellar. If you mean to fight the monster, go down and drink the wine: perchance you might vanquish him then!'

Almafi found the cellar and saw the barrel. He lifted it and took a good draught. Although he already had the strength of a thousand men, he now felt as if his muscles were made of veritable iron. He went up in search of the monster.

Almafi found the hundredth room and strode in. The monster was asleep and Almafi woke him up with a kick.

'How dare you wake me from my sleep?' asked the monster.

'Because one of us must die!' cried Almafi.

The monster was still lying down. 'I see that you are only a mortal human,' he said, 'but a brave one.' He got up and added: 'We shall put this to the test.'

He took up an iron ball, which weighed a ton. 'Whichever of us can hurl this and break that wall, shall be the victor!'

He swung it round and threw: the ball became deeply lodged in the masonry. It was Almafi's turn. He plucked the ball out and hurled it with such force that the wall parted, and the ball disappeared.

Only then did the monster take a good look at his opponent.

'I see that you are strong,' he said. 'Come, let us wrestle in the courtyard!'

And so they grappled. Almafi fought with the strength of a thousand men, but the monster with that of twelve hundred. He threw Almafi to the ground. The boy was dazed for a while but slowly got to his feet again. He faced the monster again, this time feeling that he had acquired the strength of fifteen hundred men, and flung the monster with such force that he never got up again. And so the monster gave up his wicked soul.

Almafi ran forthwith back to the girl's balcony. He declared to her:

'My dearest heart, I have been roaming round the world for more than a year to find you, and if you so will, only the spade and the great bell will ever separate us!'

By now the girl was also in love with Almafi — had he not saved her life? And was he not, after all, a most handsome young man? They swore eternal faith to each other.

Almafi wanted to stop the palace from its eternal flight, but the girl said she did not know how to halt the two mighty wings which propelled it.

'If there is no other way, I shall have to cut them off,' said he, 'if ever we see land again.'

Some days later as they sat on the balcony, Almafi sprang up.

'I can see land! What is more, I can also see a city!' It was three days before the flying palace caught up with Almafi's keen sight, and before the girl saw it too. She told Almafi that they were flying over her father's city! At this, Almafi drew his sword, and with two mighty strokes he cut off the wings of the flying palace.

When the King, below, heard a tremendous humming in the air he ran into the courtyard to see what could be causing it. Imagine his joy when he saw his daughter step down from the flying palace, accompanied by a handsome young man! There was great rejoicing and, after the King had heard the girl's story, he folded Almafi to his heart.

The King ordered that his city should be garlanded with flowers and bunting. Almafi sent for his parents and his two brothers to come to the wedding, and to settle in the city to remain near him.

There was a great celebration and they all lived happily ever after.

Almafi and the Golden Cockerel

IT was during the time of Almafi's journey, when he was seeking the weeping maiden in the flying palace. As he roamed the world for a full year, he was well equipped to face every danger. The power of the fairies had given him such vigour that hunger and thirst were strangers to him. It made his eyesight so penetrating that he could see through the clouds and to the bottom of the sea. And he had the strength of a thousand men and an invincible sword at his side. All he lacked was his heart's desire: the beautiful maiden in the flying palace!

On his way through Fairyland, one day, he came to a forest. He sat down to ponder, and presently fell asleep under a large oak tree.

He was startled by a loud *cock-a-doodle-doo!* and saw a golden-crested cock sitting on a branch overhead.

Almafi said:

'Hey-ho, my golden-crested cock, you too must be suffering from a heavy heart if you crow so sadly!'

'To be sure,' replied the cock, 'I have a sorry tale to tell.'

'Perhaps I can help you,' said Almafi encouragingly. 'Speak freely, I won't hurt you. Come down, golden cockerel, and tell me about your troubles.'

'Very well,' said the cock, and flew down to rest at Almafi's side.

'I will tell you about them, even though you will not be able to help me. Know that I was once in love with a beautiful fairy, but for my misfortune. she was also loved by the wicked Fairy of Deceit. I was a fairy prince, then, and the girl preferred me to the other, and we were engaged to be married. But on the eve of our wedding, the Fairy of Deceit sprayed me with some magic water and laid a spell on me, which turned me into the cock you now see. Only my golden crest differentiates me from ordinary cocks. So now you see why I am heavy of heart.'

'Tell me how I may retrieve your former shape for you,' said Almafi.

The cock with the golden crest explained:

'The Wicked Fairy of Deceit has a garden in which there is a well, and the well contains magic water. If you could obtain a cupful of it and spray me with it three times – without my being aware – then I would regain my former shape. I must warn you, however, that the well is guarded by a twelve-headed dragon who notices the slightest thing and pounces to devour any intruders.'

The boy remained unafraid: after all, did he not have the fairies' invincible sword? So he asked for the whereabouts of the garden with the well.

'I do not know,' said the cock, 'but the speaking mountain does. Within it is a marble board. He who finds it and reads what is written on it will be able to open the mountain's throat, and hear the human voice with which it speaks.'

'Tell me how to get there!' urged the boy.

'Tear a small piece off my crest.'

'Will it not hurt you?' asked Almafi.

'Just do as I say,' replied the cock. The boy tore a piece off, and the cock said:

'Throw it up into the air and it will fly in front of you. When it stops, you will know that you have arrived. My fortune is in your hands.'

The crest flew steadily some few feet in front of the boy, and so they travelled for three days and nights. They came to a great forest in the middle of which was a tall mountain, and the golden crest suddenly stopped its flight. Almafi knew that he had arrived.

He went within and saw the marble board, and began to read. It said that he who wished to open the mountain's throat must first bring, unaided, twelve tall pine trees from the forest below and make a bonfire with them, and when its last embers went out, the mountain would speak.

This was nothing to Almafi: he tore up twelve trees by their roots and lit a bonfire. And as the last embers went out he heard a deep rumbling voice which spoke thus:

'What is your wish, earthly mortal, who opened my throat by bringing twelve tall pine trees unaided for my bonfire?'

The boy replied:

'Tell me where is the garden of the wicked Fairy of Deceit, and what happened to the bride of the golden-crested cock?'

The mountain replied:

'There is a glass mountain under the sea and that is where the bride is held.'

'And where is the garden?'

'Go towards the East and follow the golden crest. He will show you the way.'

The crest began to move again and led Almafi, day and night, for three weeks, to the Garden of Deceit. He went in to confront the twelve-headed dragon. It bellowed so that the whole garden shook, and it breathed tongues of fire. Almafi drew his sword and found that the sword dealt its strokes as if unaided by his hand. Three heads fell at a single stroke, and the others at three more. The boy lay down to rest and fell asleep, so that he did not see the Wicked Fairy of Deceit who suddenly appeared by his side. When he woke up, Almafi found himself bound hand and foot and lying in a cellar. The Wicked Fairy sneered:

'We shall meet again in three weeks' time! That is, if you are still alive, for you shall have no food or drink meanwhile!'

But Almafi was not worried by this threat. What were three weeks without food or drink to him? He could bear it! He began to whistle.

Three weeks later the wicked Fairy of Deceit came to the cellar again. Expecting that Almafi had starved to death, he had had a great bonfire built ready to burn the body. But lo! what was this? Almafi, whistling!

He was beside himself with fury.

'I thought you had starved to death, and I was about to

burn your body. But since you are alive, I shall burn you just the same!' And he advanced on Almafi.

But the boy was quicker than the Fairy of Deceit whom he caught and tied hand and foot with his own chains and carried on to the bonfire.

'Just as you planned to burn me on the fire,' he said, 'so now you must burn yourself!'

The wicked Fairy of Deceit was burnt to ashes, and Almafi scattered these to the wind. Since when deceit has spread over the whole world.

Almafi found the well and drew a jugful of magic water from it. He turned towards the faithful little golden crest which was waiting for him, to lead him back to the forest where the golden-crested cock lived. When they arrived, the little golden crest disappeared and Almafi lay down to sleep.

A '*cock-a-doodle-doo*' woke him up next morning and he saw the cock on a branch. He said:

'Come down, golden-crested cock!'

The cock flew down and asked:

'Were you successful?'

'No,' answered the boy, 'unfortunately I was unable to reach the magic water, so I cannot help you.'

This was said in order to catch the cock unawares. The cock bowed his head sadly. Almafi quickly pulled out the jug and sprayed him three times with the magic water. The cock ruffled his feathers: he shook himself violently, and was suddenly transformed into a brave and handsome young man. He embraced Almafi and thanked him for his services.

'I know what happened to your bride,' said Almafi. 'The speaking mountain told me that she is imprisoned in a glass mountain under the sea, but it did not say where the sea was.'

'I know where it is,' replied the Fairy Prince, 'but I cannot see into its depths. So how could I possibly find her?'

'Leave that to me,' reassured Almafi. 'Let us start at once!'

For three days and three nights they travelled. The Fairy Prince possessed the power of flight, so he flew with Almafi on his back, and when he got tired they walked, and when the fairy had rested they flew again. Thus, they reached the shores of the sea.

'We have arrived,' said the Fairy Prince. 'What can you see beneath the waves?'

'Let us fly out to the middle of the sea so that I may see both shores.'

They flew out and presently Almafi said:

'I can see the glass mountain now! And I am not surprised that the wicked fairy wanted your bride for himself — she is a very beautiful girl!'

'Can you see her, then, my friend?'

'Yes, I see her,' said Almafi, 'she is combing her hair in the glass mountain. Let us return to land for I cannot help you further, as I cannot swim under the sea.'

'No matter, my friend. Leave the rest to me!' said the Fairy Prince.

And he called to a pike in the waters and asked him to collect all the other fish in the sea to help lift the glass mountain to the surface. In a short while, the mountain appeared above the waves, and when it was within reach, Almafi grabbed it and with one pull hauled it ashore. With a careful blow of his fist he shattered the glass, and the bride emerged unharmed.

It was a joyful reunion and the two lovers embraced with tenderness. They had never expected to see each other again. As they embraced again and again, a falcon circled overhead. The Fairy Prince asked him to fly to the Palace of the Fairies and take the good tidings to his mother, begging her to send a coach for them so that they could get back even more swiftly. And so they returned with Almafi to the Palace of the Fairies.

Great was the rejoicing when they arrived, and Almafi was best man at the wedding of his friend. And what a feast there was! Half the population of Fairyland was there to celebrate the happiness of their Prince and there was music and dancing for three whole days and nights. Almafi was their guest of honour and their hero. But afterwards, as all good things must come to an end, it was time for him to leave. He embraced his friend and wished him eternal happiness with his beautiful bride.

And then Almafi went forth again in search of his own destiny.

The Hedgehog

ONCE upon a time there was a poor couple. They wished to have children, but they wished in vain. As they grew older, they felt sad in the empty house. So the man bethought himself:

'Do you hear me, wife?'

'I hear you,' said his wife.

'We will go out now and walk towards the church. You will take the upper road and I the lower. Whatever we find, dog, cat or bird, we shall bring it back and rear it as our child.'

The woman agreed and they set out. She found nothing, but the man found a hedgehog. He brought it home.

'Not perhaps the most beautiful of children,' said the woman, 'but, never mind, I shall love him just the same.'

They looked after the hedgehog well, they fed him, washed him, prepared a soft bed for him, without knowing that this was no ordinary hedgehog, but a prince under a spell.

One day the hedgehog spoke up:

'Father, mother, listen to me.'

The old ones looked up. They had never seen a talking hedgehog before, and were much amazed. But, they thought, if he can speak, we might as well answer. So they asked him:

'What do you want, son?'

'Father, mother, let us buy some swine. Let us become swineherds,' said the hedgehog.

The old man sighed: 'We are too old for that kind of work. Who would drive them out?'

'I shall,' said the hedgehog.

So the old man bought the swine.

'Did you buy them?' asked the hedgehog.

'Yes, my son.'

'Very well, father. Now buy a white cock, a red cock and a black cock.'

'What do you want with those?' asked the man.

The hedgehog replied, 'With those three cocks I shall make our fortune.'

So the old man bought the cocks. When spring came, the herd had to be driven out. The old man asked:

'Who will sound the horn?'

'I will,' said the hedgehog. 'Just give me the horn, father.'

He took the horn and climbed up to the top of the house. He blew so hard that he frightened all the swine in the village. When he had finished blowing, he slid off the roof, mounted the black cock and drove the herd out into the forest. There he tied up the cock and lay down to rest himself.

That day the Black King was travelling through the forest with all his carts, all his coaches and all his household, and had lost his way. It was a great, dense forest, and when darkness fell the King was frightened. He commanded his coachman, 'Go and find someone to lead us out of here.'

So the coachman set out. He turned right, he turned left, but wherever he turned there wasn't a soul. As he wandered hither and thither he nearly trod on the hedgehog. The hedgehog was angry.

'Watch out!' he shouted. 'If you tread on me I will slap you so hard that your eyes will knock together.'

'I beg your pardon,' said the coachman.

'Lucky for you that you begged my pardon, for otherwise I would have torn you to shreds,' said the hedgehog. 'Well, who are you and what do you want?'

'I am the Black King's coachman. We have lost our way, and His Majesty asks if you could lead us out of this forest?'

'I can, if you bring me a note that the King will give me his daughter and half his kingdom in return. Without a note I won't budge, and you will all be eaten by wolves.'

'Well,' enquired the King when the coachman returned, 'did you find anyone?'

'Yes, a dangerous hedgehog.'

'I suppose he will do,' said the King.

'Yes, but he says that he will only lead us out of here if he gets an official note saying that his reward will be Your Majesty's daughter and half your kingdom.'

The Black King turned to his daughter who sat by the fire eating a baked potato.

'What do you think, my daughter?'

The beautiful Princess shrugged her shoulders.

'I would rather marry a hedgehog than be eaten up by wolves.'

So the King wrote a note, a solemn, official note with four black seals. The coachman took it back to the hedgehog. The hedgehog pocketed the note and led the King out of the great, dense forest.

Thereupon the hedgehog returned to his herd and drove it home. Then he said, 'Father, feed the red cock well tomorrow, because I shall need him.'

Next morning the hedgehog blew on his horn, mounted the red cock and drove his herd out into the forest. There, he tied up the cock and lay down to rest himself.

That day the Red King was travelling through the forest with all his carts, all his coaches and all his household. He was still travelling when darkness fell – so dark, that ahead or behind he couldn't tell t'other from which.

The Red King gave a great cry. 'Coachman, come here!'

The coachman came and asked respectfully how he might serve the King.

'Go,' said the King, 'go and find someone to lead us out of here.'

So the coachman set out. He turned left, he turned right, but wherever he turned there wasn't a ghost of a soul. As he wandered anxiously hither and thither, he almost trod on the hedgehog. The hedgehog was angry and started to shout.

'Watch out! If you tread on me I will slap you so hard that your eyes will knock together.'

'I beg your pardon,' said the coachman.

'Lucky for you that you begged my pardon, for

e I would have torn you to shreds,' growled the
g. 'Well, who are you and what do you want?'
he Red King's coachman. We have lost our way,
His Majesty asks if you could lead us out of the forest?'

'I can, if you bring me a note that the King will give me
his daughter and half his kingdom in return. Without a
note I won't budge, and you will all be eaten by wolves
before it is day.'

The coachman returned to his master.

'Well,' enquired the King, 'did you find anyone?'

'Yes, a dangerous hedgehog.'

'I suppose he will do,' said the King.

'Yes, but he says he will only lead us out of here if he
gets an official note saying that his reward will be Your
Majesty's daughter and half your kingdom.'

The Red King turned to his daughter who sat by the fire
eating nuts.

'What do you think, my daughter?'

The lovely Princess looked up.

'I would rather marry a hedgehog any day than be eaten
up by wolves.'

So the King wrote a note, a solemn, official note with
four red seals. The coachman took it to the hedgehog. The
hedgehog pocketed the note and led the King out of the
great, dense forest.

Thereupon the hedgehog returned to his herd and drove
it home. Then he said, 'Father, feed the white cock well
tomorrow, because I shall need him.'

Next morning, at dawn, the hedgehog blew on his
horn, leapt on the white cock's back and drove his herd out
into the forest. There he tied up the cock and lay down to
rest himself.

That day, the White King was travelling through the
forest. When it got dark he was so lost that he couldn't tell

whether he was coming or going. So he called his coachman and ordered him to look for someone to lead them out
of this great, dense forest.

The coachman set out to search the dark forest.
Whether he turned right or left, there was not a shaft of
light nor any sign of a human. As he wandered aimlessly
hither and thither, he nearly trod on the hedgehog. The
hedgehog shouted in anger:

'Watch out! If you tread on me I will slap you so hard
that your eyes will knock together.'

'I beg your pardon,' said the coachman.

'Lucky for you that you begged my pardon, for otherwise I would have torn you to shreds,' growled the hedgehog. 'Well, who are you and what do you want?'

'I am the White King's coachman. We have lost our
way, and His Majesty asks if you could lead us out of this
forest?'

'I can, if you bring me a note that the King will give me
his daughter and half his kingdom in return. Without a
note I won't budge, and you will all be eaten by wolves
before it is day.'

The coachman returned to his master.

'Well,' enquired the King, 'did you find anyone?'

'Yes, a dangerous hedgehog.'

'He might help us just the same,' said the King.

'Yes, but he says he will only lead us out of here if he
gets an official note saying that his reward will be your
Majesty's daughter and half your kingdom.'

The White King turned to his daughter who was frying
pancakes on the fire.

'What do you think, my daughter?'

The beautiful Princess bowed her head. 'For my father's
sake I shall gladly marry, even a hedgehog.'

So the King wrote a note, a solemn, official note with

four white seals. The coachman took it to the hedgehog. The hedgehog pocketed the note and led the King out of the great, dense forest.

Thereupon the hedgehog returned to his herd and drove it home. Then he spoke to his father: 'Know, my father, that I have made our fortune. Sell your worries and buy a coach-and-four with the price. I wish to get married and I am off to seek my bride.'

'To seek your bride, my son?' marvelled the poor man. 'But there isn't a single hedgehog in this neighbourhood.'

The hedgehog shook his head. 'What do you take me for, father? I don't wish to marry a hedgehog, but a princess.'

Well, the poor man sold his worries and he bought a coach-and-six with the price. The hedgehog got into the coach and didn't stop until he reached the Black King's palace. There he jumped out and knocked on the door.

A sentry appeared and asked, 'Who and what are you and what is your business?'

The hedgehog explained that he had a letter from the King and he had come to collect the Princess and half the kingdom too, provided there was room in his satchel for it.

'Wait here,' said the sentry, 'I will announce you.' With that he slouched off. The hedgehog waited for an hour. He waited for two hours; he waited for three. But he had no patience for more. So he unhitched one of his horses, leapt over the castle walls and rode straight into the throne-room.

When the Black King saw him he turned as green as an unripe apple.

'Is this your gratitude?' asked the hedgehog. 'I led you out of the forest and saved you from being eaten by wolves and now you greet me with locked doors! I am a bride-groom, not a beggar!'

The Black King realized there was no point in arguing, sighed greatly and asked, 'Will you get married here or at home?'

'I want to get married where I was baptized,' replied the hedgehog.

'Very well, then,' grunted the Black King, 'take my

daughter and take her dowry. You will have to return for half the kingdom after the wedding.'

Then the Black King gave orders that his daughter's dowry should be laden in a cart. The servants loaded thirteen carts with gold, silver, silks and velvets.

The hedgehog placed his bride by his side on the box of the coach. When they were some distance from the palace, the hedgehog turned to the Princess.

'My sweet bride, do you love me?'

'Do I love you? I don't want to see you until I can see my own back!'

The hedgehog pulled the reins and the coach stopped.

'Well,' said the hedgehog to the Princess, 'if you don't love me, you may go home.'

The Princess jumped promptly to the ground. 'And what about my dowry?' she questioned.

'I shall take that home as payment for leading you out of the forest.'

When he reached home, the hedgehog packed the vast treasure into the lumber-room. He stabled the horses, had supper and then said:

'My dear parents, there's money, but no bride. I'll get one tomorrow. If not tomorrow, then the day after.'

At dawn next morning he got into the coach again and didn't stop until he reached the Red King's country. Soon he found the royal palace too. He would have entered but the door was locked. He banged it. When he banged three times, a sleepy sentry shuffled out. 'Who and what are you and what is your business?'

The hedgehog explained that he had a letter from the King and he had come to collect the Princess and half the kingdom too, provided there was room in his satchel for it.

'Wait here,' said the sentry, 'I will tell the King!' With that he shambled off. The hedgehog waited for an hour.

He waited for two hours; he waited for three. But he had no patience for more. He unhitched one of his horses, leapt over the castle walls and rode straight into the throne-room.

When the Red King saw him he turned as yellow as a sick lemon.

'Is this your gratitude?' asked the hedgehog. 'I led you out of the forest and saved you from being eaten by wolves and now you greet me with locked doors! I am a bride-groom, not a beggar!'

The Red King realized there was no point in arguing, sighed in resignation and asked, 'Will you get married here or at home?'

'I want to get married where I was baptized,' replied the hedgehog.

'Very well then,' groaned the Red King, 'take my daughter and take her dowry. I shall forward half the kingdom by post.'

Then he ordered that his daughter's dowry should be laden in a cart. The servants loaded thirteen carts with gold, silver, silks, velvets and pork cracklings.

The hedgehog placed his bride by his side on the box of the coach. When they were some distance from the palace, the hedgehog turned to the Princess.

'My sweet bride, do you love me?'

'I love you as I love rotten marrows or dead toads!'

'Well,' said the hedgehog to the Princess, 'if you don't love me, you may go home.'

The Princess jumped nimbly to the ground. 'And what about my dowry?' she demanded.

'I shall take that home as payment for leading you out of the forest.'

When he reached home, the hedgehog packed the vast treasure into the attic. He stabled the horses, had supper and then he said, 'My dear parents, there's money again, but still no bride. I shall get one tomorrow. But if I don't get one, then do not expect me home again.'

The old couple wept and tried to persuade him every this way and that to come home just the same but the hedgehog stuck to his words. At dawn next morning he got into the coach again and didn't stop until he reached the White King's country. He saw the royal palace too, glinting white from afar, like snow.

He drove up – and the door was open wide. He drove in – and the White King himself came running to welcome him.

'At last you've arrived, my dear son! We've been waiting for you. Will you get married here or at home?'

'If it is your pleasure, Your Majesty, here.'

What a feast there was! Three hundred oxen were roasted, not to mention a great many pigs, geese, ducks and turkeys. After the wedding the carts were laden with the bride's dowry. The bride sat at the side of the hedgehog on the box of the coach.

When they were some distance from the palace, the hedgehog turned to the Princess.

'My sweet wife, do you love me?'

The Princess stroked the hedgehog's head gently and said:

'I do love you, of course I love you!'

At that very instant the hedgehog turned into a handsome young prince! He was so very, very, very handsome that the Princess broke into tears of joy, the six horses pulling their coach took fright and didn't stop until they reached the old couple's home.

There the Prince-That-Used-To-Be-A-Hedgehog declared that he had been under a spell and that he was changed back by the sweet words of the Princess. The old couple were joyful that their hedgehog son had turned into such a fine lad. They rejoiced with the new bride, too. They are rejoicing still, if they are still alive.

Ever Thus and As You Were

ONCE upon a time, somewhere, closer than near, further than far, there was a soldier. Having served his time he obtained his discharge and returned home. He could have lived happily if only he had some money or some land. But he had neither. So, after a lot of hard thinking he went to see the King.

The King lived in a beautiful palace at the far end of the village. There was a sentry at the door and the soldier told him that he wished to see the King.

'Wait here and I'll announce you,' replied the sentry.

He duly reported that a discharged soldier wished to see His Majesty.

'Let him enter,' said the King.

The soldier knocked politely and when he heard the King say, 'Come in,' he entered. He saluted the King and then told him his business.

'I am a discharged soldier, Your Majesty, and I come to seek employment at your court.'

After some thought the King said:

'I need a coachman, my son. But first you must prove to me that you can drive well.'

'I'll prove it,' promised the soldier.

So the King took the soldier down to the stables. Two miserable nags stood by the manger. They were so feeble that their legs could hardly support their own weight.

'Well, my son,' said the King, 'harness these horses and drive the cart out to the royal forest. If you can bring me back a load of timber with these horses, I will believe that you can drive and I'll make you my coachman.'

The soldier harnessed the two horses and took his place on the box of the cart. He drove out through the gates of the palace. The miserable nags went jogging along but their thin legs kept knocking together. The soldier realized that even their own weight was too much for them, so he dismounted and followed on foot.

It was dusk by the time he reached the royal wood. The soldier found the woodman who showed him the timber. He loaded the cart and was ready to drive back. He urged the horses on but to no effect. The poor nags tried their best, but the cart stuck fast.

So the soldier applied his shoulders to the cart and pushed it from behind, moving it slowly forward. He was a strong man but even so he was soon soaked in sweat.

When they reached the main road he sat down for a rest, and to rest the horses too.

As he sat there, panting, he saw an old man approach.

'Good-day,' said the old man.

'Good-day, Sir,' replied the soldier, politely.

'I am very tired,' complained the old man, 'I can hardly walk. Allow me to sit on your cart.'

The soldier thought that the cart and the timber were already heavy enough for the horses. But he felt sorry for the old man. He was so old, so weak, that he couldn't be left at the roadside.

'Take a seat, Sir,' he said.

The old man took his place on the box and said to the soldier:

'Come, my son, sit by me and we can start.'

'We can start certainly,' replied the soldier, 'but I won't sit by you because the horses are weak and I must push the cart.'

'Come, have no fear. There is no need to push the cart. I will drive and you will soon see how quickly we can reach the village.'

The soldier wagged his head.

'Well, Sir, if you think you can drive better than me, then let us try, by all means!'

With that he sat on the box. The old man took the reins and said to the horses, in a quiet voice:

'*Ever thus.*'

As soon as they heard this, the horses tossed their heads. They moved off with such lightning speed that they looked more like magic steeds than tired old nags. In his astonishment the soldier nearly fell off the box! He was still amazed as they reached the outskirts of the village. When the old man stopped the horses he said:

'Well, here we are, my son. You've done me a good deed

and, as a reward, I will invest you with my knowledge. If you heed my advice you will become the best coachman in the whole wide world. No matter what poor nags you drive – even dead ones if you like – all you need to say is: '*Ever thus*' – and they will move off like the wind. And when you want them to stop, just say: '*As you were.*'

The soldier wanted to thank the old man, but there was nobody to thank. There was no one by his side, and he saw no one around. The old man had vanished into thin air.

The soldier then decided to try out his new-found knowledge. He took the reins and said:

'*Ever thus.*'

Immediately the cart moved off, as if through air, like the wind. The King was at the palace window to see the soldier return with the timber. When he saw the two miserable nags galloping along he was astounded. He saw the cart turning into the palace yard.

'*As you were,*' said the soldier and the horses stopped.

The King was full of praise.

'Well, my son, you are truly a born coachman. I am an old man but I have never seen such driving. I shall keep my promise. I appoint you as my coachman. You won't have to cart manure or groom the horses – it will be enough if you drive. You will live well: you deserve it.'

Then the King showed the soldier his quarters. He gave him new clothes, new boots, and ordered that he should bring round the coach next morning for a drive.

Next morning, the soldier drove the coach to the entrance of the palace. The great doors opened. The King and Queen appeared, followed by the three Princesses, one more beautiful than the other. The soldier's eyes immediately fastened on the youngest and he resolved that he would either marry this girl or no one. The royal family took their places in the coach and the soldier tugged the

reins. He allowed the horses to trot quietly until they
reached the edge of the village. Then he whispered:

'*Ever thus.*'

The horses sprang to and the coach flew down the road as
if through the air! The three Princesses shrieked with joy,
their hair streamed in the wind, their faces became rosy.
The soldier drove back to the palace yard and whispered:

'*As you were.*'

The coach stopped instantly. The King was full of praise for the soldier; since the beginning of the world he had never met such a coachman! He asked him to lunch, he asked him to dinner. The soldier ate and drank his fill and walked about the palace as proudly as a prince.

However, despite all these honours, when he was alone he felt sad. He knew well that it would be useless to ask for the hand of the youngest Princess; the King would never permit it. A coachman cannot marry a princess.

He was saddest of all the day when the suitors arrived. Princes came and dukes, counts galore and barons. Each princess chose a bridegroom for herself and half the county was invited to celebrate the engagements. The soldier was one of the servants and great was his sorrow as he walked about the dazzling halls.

Then he noticed the youngest Princess and her bridegroom having a meal. He sneaked up behind them and whispered:

'*Ever thus.*'

In that instant the Princess and the bridegroom began to eat so fast that those beside them stared in disbelief. The servants brought them dish after dish. The pair went on eating, they grew visibly fatter and fatter until they could hardly move in their chairs.

The Queen happened to pass by. When she saw them, she scolded them severely:

'Aren't you ashamed of yourselves, eating like this? Haven't you any manners? Are you starvelings or royalty? Stop at once, or you'll be sorry!'

Thus she gabbled on, and at the height of her gabbling, the soldier bent over and whispered to her:

'*Ever thus.*'

At that, words were veritably tumbling out of the

Queen so that nothing could be heard in the entire palace except her voice!

The King saw what was happening. He came to the Queen to silence her. He was about to speak when he hiccuped.

'*Ever thus*,' whispered the soldier, and the King continued to hiccup so much that he bit each word in two. He was frightened and shouted:

'I am ill – hic! – call the doctor – hic! – I shall die – hic!'

The doctor arrived and just as he was about to examine the king, he sneezed.

'*Ever thus*,' said the soldier, and the wretched doctor began to sneeze again and again.

But the King heard what the soldier had said and realized that he was the cause of all this trouble. He spoke to the general:

'General – hic! – cut down the coachman – hic! – or we die – hic!'

The general drew his sword. The soldier wasn't a soldier for nothing and he struck the sword out of the general's hand. When the general bent down to pick it up, the soldier gave a great shout:

'*Ever thus!*'

The general kept bending, the Queen kept gabbling, the King kept hiccuping, the doctor kept sneezing and the Princess and the bridegroom kept eating!

The King realized that force was useless. He began to entreat:

'Have pity on us soldier – hic! – cure us – hic! – I give you half my kingdom – hic!'

'I don't want half your kingdom, Sire,' said the soldier, it's enough if you give me your youngest daughter.'

The King turned to his daughter.

'Will you – hic! – take – hic! – the soldier, –hic! – my daughter? – hic!'

'Of course,' replied the Princess between two mouthfuls, 'if only I could stop eating!'

The King turned to the bridegroom.

'And you – hic! – will you give up – hic! – my daughter? – hic!'

'Certainly, if only I could stop eating!'

The soldier stretched out his hand and the King took it.

As they shook hands on the deal, the soldier said to the King:

'*As you were!*'

His Majesty's hiccups ceased at once. Then the soldier lifted the magic from each in turn. The Queen stopped gabbling, the doctor stopped sneezing, the general stopped bending, the youngest Princess and her former bridegroom stopped eating.

And the soldier married the youngest Princess.

'Are you happy?' he asked her.

'Very happy,' answered the youngest Princess.

Upon which the soldier simply said:

'*Ever thus.*'

And since he was never to say '*as you were*,' the two of them lived happily ever after.

A Dragon-tale

ONCE upon a time, in one of the smaller countries of Fairyland, there lived a poor man who had two sons. They were both well-set, handsome young men, but there the resemblance ended. Istvan, the eldest, was bad-tempered and morose, selfish and lazy. Janos, the youngest, was good-tempered and cheerful, generous and kind.

'There goes Istvan,' the old man would remark when he saw his eldest son idling around, 'the boy will remain a beggar to his dying day. Whereas you, my son, will be rich.'

'Not so, father,' Janos would reply, 'because what I have I shall always share with my brother.'

One fine day, the King of their country issued a proclamation. It stated that any man who could liberate the Princess from her troubles would receive her hand in marriage and half the kingdom as her dowry.

The unfortunate Princess was indeed in dire trouble. She was first courted by a seven-headed copper dragon, and then by a seven-headed iron dragon. The copper dragon had seated himself one day by her side and had announced:

'I shall not move from here until you consent to become my wife.'

Similarly, the iron dragon had taken a seat on her other side, declaring:

'I swear I shall remain here until you consent to become my wife.'

The Princess had no wish to assume the condition of a dragon's wife and had resolutely refused to consent to either. So the two dragons remained where they sat, watching over each other and guarding the Princess. What was even worse, they had changed her into a dragon, too, for greater safety. A visitor to the throne-room would have observed a sorrowing King, weeping on his throne, and, on the other side of the room, three identical dragons sitting close together in a row, also bathed in tears!

When the poor old man heard the King's proclamation he spoke to his eldest son Istvan:

'You are not much use here at home because of your idleness. Go and try your fortune — you may even gain half the kingdom!'

With much grumbling and groaning, Istvan prepared for the journey and set out. He made his way through a dark forest and trudged across a silken meadow. He became so tired that he sat down to eat the cakes which he had brought with him. While he ate, he noticed a whole colony of ants crawling towards the crumbs on the ground. This irritated him so much that he swept up the crumbs, put his cakes back into his satchel, got up, and, with a bad-tempered kick at the anthill, walked away.

Muttering and grumbling to himself as he went, he came to a lake where twelve golden ducklings were disporting themselves in the blue water. The sight of them annoyed Istvan so much that he grabbed a handful of pebbles and threw them at the ducklings. They were startled and swam away, leaving their jollity behind.

Having given way to his temper, Istvan calmed down somewhat. He increased his pace and, by the following morning, he arrived at the royal castle. He knocked at the door and an ugly old crone opened the spy-hole.

'What have you come for, my young lad?' she croaked.

'To liberate the Princess,' he answered.

The old crone opened the door and sprinkled a sackful of millet on the ground in front of Istvan.

'Gather it up, my son,' she urged, 'because this is the first of your three tests!'

Istvan would have done so, but for a whole regiment of ants which suddenly appeared and ate all the millet up in a trice.

He spent the rest of the day knocking at the door but it remained shut as if for ever.

However, next morning the spy-hole opened again and, when the old crone saw Istvan, she opened the door, pulled out twelve golden keys and threw them across into the lake opposite.

'Find me those keys, my son,' she called, 'because this is your second test.'

Istvan took his clothes off and plunged into the lake. He spent the rest of the day in the water, digging and rummaging for the keys in the mud below, but in vain.

Next morning, he kicked the door so furiously that the whole castle echoed to his temper.

'There is nothing for you here!' said the old crone, opening the spy-hole. 'You failed the tests and I advise you to go home quietly.'

Istvan objected that there was a third test and that he would not give up at this stage. He argued so stubbornly that the crone opened the door at last and led him up to the throne-room. Istvan saw the King sitting on his throne, tears streaming down his sad face, and the three dragons on the other side, sitting side by side, also weeping.

'Tell me, which of those three is the Princess?' demanded the crone.

It is a difficult matter to decide which of three identical dragons is a false dragon. Istvan was quite unable to tell them apart and pointed at random.

'That one is the Princess!'

He was wrong.

Instantly, the two real dragons roared out and, answering their call, a giant appeared. He grabbed Istvan, dragged him outside and threw him to the ground. The ground opened and instantly swallowed him up.

The old man at home waited long for the return of his son. When his last hope had faded, he spoke to his youngest son, Janos:

'Go and try your fortune too.'

Janos took his satchel and made his way through the dark forest. He, too, sat down in the silken meadow to eat his cakes, and soon the ants began to swarm round the crumbs. When he saw how hungry the poor creatures were, Janos crumbled up a cake and scattered it — let them have a real feast, he thought. Some of the ants ate so much that they staggered about. This made Janos smile and he continued on his journey whistling a merry tune.

He was still whistling when he saw the lake with the twelve golden ducklings swimming around. They all turned to face him and he wondered what they wanted?

'Of course!' he thought. 'They must be hungry, too.' He distributed the rest of his cakes between the twelve ducklings, who ate them with evident relish, accompanied by a lot of grateful quacks, as if to say that Janos had been their rescuer.

Next morning, he arrived at the castle and knocked on the door. The spy-hole opened and the ugly old crone looked out enquiringly.

'What have you come for, my son?' she asked.

'To liberate the Princess,' he answered.

The old crone sprinkled a sackful of millet on the ground.

'Gather it up, my son,' she said, 'because this is your first test.'

Janos had begun to do so, but he did not succeed either; because a whole regiment of ants had gathered it up for him and had filled the sack in a trice. Janos tied the sack securely and called to the crone that her millet was safely gathered.

Without saying a word, the old crone threw the twelve golden keys into the lake opposite and indicated, with a nod of her head, that Janos should return them to her.

He began to undress, but before he had pulled off his shirt, he saw twelve golden ducklings marching towards him, each with a golden key in its beak.

Janos again called to the crone that the keys had been found.

'I know, my dear,' she said from behind the door. Janos was curious:

'How did you know?'

'Simply because I have just been changed from an ugly old crone into a young fairy princess. I have been a servant in this castle for the last three hundred years. But you have lifted the wicked curse from my head by your kindness to the ants and the ducklings. You helped me, and now I shall help you.'

The Fairy Princess opened the door. She was still wearing the ragged clothes of the old crone, but her beauty shone out. There were tears in Janos's eyes as though he had looked at the sun.

'There are three dragons inside the castle,' explained the Fairy Princess, 'and you must look for the one which rests its seventh head in its lap. That one is the Princess. Here is a sword with which you must slay the other two dragons. Having done so, you must put on this pin-encrusted suit and return to the spot where you are now standing. You will stamp the ground three times. A giant will appear who holds your brother in thrall. Trust him to do the rest.'

Without another word, the Fairy Princess took wing and flew up into the clouds. She had been away from her parents for three hundred years, which is a long time even in Fairyland.

Janos grasped the sword and entered the throne-room. The King was still weeping on one side of the room, and the three dragons on the other.

'Which is my daughter, young man?' asked the King, sobbing.

'Who else,' replied Janos, pointing, 'but the one with her seventh head in her lap.'

Saying this he drew his sword and struck at the other two dragons in turn. With fourteen mighty blows he cut off their heads and their lives.

When at last he looked at the third dragon, he saw a beautiful young princess instead. He left her to rejoice

with her father and ran back to the main door of the castle. He donned the pin-encrusted suit, then he stepped out and stamped three times. The ground opened up and the giant leaned out. He was so huge that his mouth was the size of an oven and his teeth resembled anvils.

'What do you want, you impertinent worm?' thundered the giant. 'I will gobble you up instantly!'

And this is exactly what he did, except that the pins on Janos's suit pricked every part of the giant's mouth most painfully! He couldn't bear to swallow him. He couldn't bear to spit him out either, and he couldn't bear to bite him, because Janos sat on his tongue. In the end, the giant entreated him thus:

'I will be your life-long servant, I will pray for you to the end of your days, but please come out of my mouth!'

'Before I do,' replied Janos, 'you must satisfy my three demands. First, release my brother!'

'I release him!' groaned the giant. He reached into the chasm behind him and placed the unharmed Istvan on the ground.

'Promise, with a sacred oath,' continued Janos, 'that you will depart from hence and settle somewhere else!'

'I promise!' croaked the giant.

'My third demand,' went on Janos, 'is that you procure two beams for me.'

The giant found two beams and Janos propped the giant's mouth open, just in case the fiend had a mind to bite him in two. Then he jumped nimbly to the ground.

'Go and grow taller!' joked Janos, dismissing the giant with a wave of the hand, and he took off the pin-encrusted suit. The fiend crept out of the chasm and slunk away in defeat, and hasn't been heard of since.

Janos took his brother's hand and they entered the castle. They found the Princess and her royal father in each other's arms, this time with tears of joy in their eyes. When she saw her rescuer, the Princess flew into Janos's arms and they kissed each other tenderly. They were married that very day.

A great feast was held and half the population of that small country was invited to the celebrations. Janos sent for his father who was asked to stay with them for the rest of his life. And Istvan, the elder brother, who had learnt his lesson in that terrible chasm, became good-tempered and generous. In fact, if you happen to be in the vicinity of that castle in Fairyland, you will see him feeding the ants and ducklings every day!

The Cauldron of Gold

ONCE upon a time there was a poor man. He had a great many children and, naturally enough, they all had to be fed. True, he had a pair of small cows as well, but how could two small cows support such a big family? Consequently, the poor man and his family were more often hungry than not, and he spent the live-long day sighing and moaning about his poverty, his difficulties and life in general. If only some good fortune would come his way to make their lot easier, he sighed. And he kept on sighing until one day when good fortune did, indeed, come his way.

He was ploughing his field as it happened, when suddenly the ploughshare got stuck on something and his two small cows couldn't move forward any more, however hard they tried. The poor man bent down to see what was obstructing his plough and he nearly choked in amazement. Lying in the furrow was a cauldron: an enormous cauldron filled to the brim with gold! The poor man was so delighted with his good fortune that he didn't know whether he was standing on his head or his heels.

A little later on he was still undecided as to what he should do next. Should he leave the little cows in the field? No, they might be stolen. Should he drive home, cows and plough and all? No, the neighbours might be suspicious.

As he sat there worrying over his problems this way and that, who should come his way but a discharged soldier. He saw the cauldron of gold and practically fell over with surprise.

'That's some treasure, if I'm not mistaken,' he said.

'Some treasure, indeed,' agreed the poor man.

'What are you doing with this gold here?' asked the soldier.

'I'm worrying about it,' replied the poor man. 'I can't leave it here and I can't take it home by myself. Oh dear, what should I do, what should I do?'

The soldier began to worry about the problem himself, pacing up and down over the furrows. What indeed, what indeed? – he kept muttering. At last he heard the poor man say:

'If I could find someone to carry the cauldron back home for me, I wouldn't begrudge him a fistful of gold.'

The soldier stopped pacing. 'For a fistful of gold I'll carry it myself,' he volunteered. And so it was agreed.

The poor man gave him a fistful of gold, and the soldier lifted up the heavy cauldron. He grunted as he lifted it on to his shoulder, and he groaned with each step he took. Eventually, however, he reached the crossroads not far from the village.

He put his heavy burden down and sat by the ditch to rest. He was still panting and groaning. But when he got his breath back he bethought himself. Why should he carry the cauldron back to the poor man's house? Why shouldn't he keep the cauldron to himself, gold and all?

He got up. He took his jacket off and spread it over the cauldron. He shouldered it once again and continued to walk. But this time he took the other road instead, the one which led towards the town.

When he reached the town at last, he made straight for the inn. He hired a room and hid the cauldron under the bed. Then he went downstairs and ordered some food from the innkeeper. After which he ordered a drink — and then he ordered some more drink. The fat innkeeper could hardly keep up and his legs were practically worn out with running to fetch these continuous orders.

The poor man, meanwhile, returned home. He was rubbing his hands with glee and kept winking at his children as he asked:

'Well, where's the great big cauldron, hey? Where's the great big cauldron?'

He could have asked a hundred times but the children hadn't seen even the ghost of a cauldron in the house.

The poor man stopped rubbing his hands. Suddenly he was alarmed.

'How's that? Didn't the soldier come? Didn't he bring the cauldron of gold?' he asked, trembling like a leaf.

'No,' replied the children, 'no soldier came to this house, and nobody brought any gold in cauldrons or even baskets.'

The poor man was beside himself with grief. It hurt to

think that the soldier had cheated him so badly, and it hurt even more that everything was again as before and that there would be no end to their poverty after all.

The children questioned him and he told them how he had found the cauldron of gold and how the soldier had offered to bring it home for him. And now, misery, there was no sign of either the soldier or the cauldron!

Amongst his many children there were three girls who were almost grown up. The eldest was called Bring-mewyne, the middle one was Hadenuff and the youngest was Irunaweigh. They were smart, clever girls, all three of them, and they wanted to help their father.

'Don't worry, father,' said the youngest, 'because the three of us will find that mean soldier and bring back the cauldron of gold to you!'

They set out straight away and went to the town, guessing that the soldier would have gone there and would be staying at the inn. In no time at all they spotted him. There he sat among all his bottles: his nose was as red as a pepper, his ears were as red as beetroot and his face was as red as a carrot. It must have been all the red wine that had coloured him so cruelly.

As soon as he noticed the three girls he asked them politely to join him at his table. The girls accepted his invitation and, according to custom, they shook hands, and introduced themselves:

'My name is Danny Drinkalott,' he said.

'And mine is Bringmewyne,' said the eldest girl.

'Mine is Hadenuff,' said the middle girl.

'And mine is Irunaweigh,' said the youngest girl.

They sat down and chatted with him until it was evening. By that time the soldier had had some further bottles brought to him and, as a result, he hardly knew his mouth from his ear. The girls were waiting for just this

moment. Two of them stood up and supported the soldier up to his room, and while they helped him to bed, the youngest girl found the cauldron, spread her scarf over it and took it downstairs. The other two girls said good-bye to the soldier:

'If you need anything just call us – we are sleeping in the next room.'

'Yes, I'll call you,' muttered the soldier and promptly fell asleep.

But he woke up at dawn with a dreadful ache in his stomach. He remembered what the eldest girl had said and he shouted for her:

'Bringmewyne!'

The innkeeper had heard the shout, too, and called back:

'Bring me wine, is it? All right then, I'll fetch it at once!'

And he went down to the cellar to get a bottle.

The soldier thought that the eldest girl couldn't have heard his call, so he shouted for the middle girl:

'Hadenuff! Hadenuff!'

He was still calling her name as the innkeeper reached his door with a bottle of wine.

'Well,' he said through the door, 'I certainly agree that you've had enough!' And he returned to the cellar.

Meanwhile, the soldier was getting impatient because neither of the two girls seemed to have heard his calls. So he called even louder for the youngest girl:

'Irunaweigh! Irunaweigh!'

Hearing this, the innkeeper turned and ran back to the soldier's door. He was angry and began to shout:

'If you shout "I run away" and you think that you can run away without paying, then you have another thought coming!'

The soldier jumped out of bed and called to the innkeeper:

'Don't you shout at me, innkeeper! If you go on shouting I'll buy this whole wretched inn from you!' He was boasting about his newly stolen wealth beneath the bed.

He bent down to reach for the cauldron. Nothing! He reached further back. Nothing! He dropped to his hands and knees to look under the bed. Nothing! The cauldron had vanished! The girls! It must have been the three girls!

'Where are they?' he shouted to the innkeeper.

'Who?' asked the innkeeper.

'Bringmewyne, Hadenuff and Irunaweigh,' said the soldier.

Hearing this, the innkeeper pushed the door open and entered. He spoke menacingly:

'The "bring me wine" was your demand; the "had enough" was just as well, but the "I run away" will not come off! Because if you think of running away without first paying me, I will first pay you off with this stick!'

With which he belaboured the soldier to his heart's content.

When he got tired of it he asked, 'Well, soldier, do you still want to run away?'

'I do,' groaned the soldier, 'but I can hardly crawl.'

And that is how he left the inn, on all fours, and he is probably crawling still.

The three girls had, meanwhile, taken the cauldron of gold back to their father. And he bought a house for each of his children, and gave them each some gold to spare.

Goosy Gander

ONCE upon a time there was a poor young man whose name was Matty Gander. He lived in a small hut by the side of a meadow and he had a flock of geese, but besides these he had very little else. So he spent his days looking after his geese in the meadow.

There came a time when Matty needed some money, so he decided to take six of his geese to market. He would sell them at their proper price of two crowns a pair. Then he

would have six crowns which would be enough for all his
needs. He therefore packed a satchel and drove his six geese
to the neighbouring town of Dobrog.

Now, Dobrog was a fine town and it had a fine market.
The people of Dobrog were fine too – all, that is, except
one of them. And that one was the Squire of Dobrog. He
was a cruel and selfish man who ruled the town as if all the
people only existed for his own personal use. As he was a
powerful man the people of Dobrog went in fear of him
every day of their lives.

Arriving at the market, Matty settled down to wait for a
customer to buy his geese. He had not long to wait either,
because a man came and stopped in front of him. Matty
looked up and saw that it was none other than the Squire of
Dobrog himself.

'How much a pair for these geese of yours?' he demanded.

Matty Gander was not afraid of the Squire and he spoke
boldly.

'Two crowns a pair, which is their proper price.'

The Squire was incensed by Matty's boldness. 'What's
this? Who are you, you miserable goosy gallows-fodder to
charge me such a price? Me, the Squire of this town! I shall
pay twopence a pair or else!'

'Then I shall not sell them to you,' replied Matty
calmly. 'The price is two crowns a pair as I said.'

Two soldiers stood behind the Squire of Dobrog. He
gave them an order. 'Arrest this man and take him back to
my house. Bring the geese as well.'

So the soldiers took Matty to the Squire's house. The
Squire got the geese for nothing – or to be more precise,
he ordered the soldiers to give Matty twenty-five strokes of
the birch in payment for them!

'Very well,' said Matty Gander as soon as he had

regained his breath from the birching, 'but just you wait, I shall repay you three times for this!'

Hearing which the Squire became so furious that he promptly ordered another twenty-five strokes! Then the soldiers released Matty at last. He went without another word and whatever he may have thought he kept to himself.

And so a year went by. It was hard for Matty without money but he managed somehow. And all the while he had remembered the Squire's cruelty, nor had his anger at the Squire's cruelty left him. So one day when he heard that the Squire of Dobrog was having a new palace built, Matty had an idea. He disguised himself as a carpenter and went off to see the new palace. There it stood, half-built already, and there was a pile of timber on the ground waiting to be used for the other half. Matty went over to the pile and inspected it like any master-carpenter.

When the Squire of Dobrog saw him he thought that some foreign carpenter had arrived and he was curious. He came out and asked Matty (whom he did not recognize) who and what he was.

'I am a master-carpenter from foreign parts,' replied Matty, 'and quite well known even if I say so myself.'

'In that case can you tell me if this timber is good enough?' The Squire was anxious about his new palace and he wanted the best.

'If you want my opinion,' said Matty after some consideration, 'this timber is not up to standard. It would be a pity to spoil your new palace with it.'

The Squire pondered for a while and then he said: 'I have a forest here and it contains some excellent trees. If this timber is not suitable I can have some better ones cut. Come with me, and choose the best!' And he ordered a hundred axe-men to come with them, and got into his coach with Matty at his side.

When they reached the forest they got out and Matty proceeded to inspect the trees. He marked the best ones for the axe-men, and led the Squire deeper and deeper into the forest in search of some more. As they proceeded, so some axe-men stayed behind to cut down the marked trees, and as they went deeper still they came to a dark dell and found themselves all alone. Matty and the Squire could hardly hear the sound of the axes way behind them.

Matty found a suitable tree and spoke. 'Will you measure the girth of that tree? I think it will serve.'

The Squire of Dobrog embraced the tree to see how thick it was. And that was the moment Matty had been waiting for. Quick as a flash he skipped round to the other side and tied the Squire's wrists together with some twine. Then he cut himself a goodly cane and with it he proceeded to repay the Squire for the beating he had himself been given. He beat him so well that the Squire was quite unable to shout for help: all he could do was to revolve his eyes in agonized surprise.

When Matty had finished with the cane at last he said:

'I am not a carpenter at all. I am Matty Gander! Remember? The goosy one. Goosy Gander, and that is my name from now on. I am the one from whom you stole the geese. The one whom you had beaten up. And I shall come twice more because I promised to repay you three times and I still owe you two more beatings!'

With which Goosy Gander turned and walked away. The Squire of Dobrog was left there still embracing his tree, gasping for breath and more dead than alive. Meanwhile, the axe-men had finished their work and they sat down to wait for the Squire and the carpenter to return. After a long time, as there was no sign of them they went in search and combed the forest until nightfall. At last they found the Squire embracing a tree and still gasping for breath. But there was no sign of the carpenter. The Squire could hardly speak.

'Help!' he croaked. 'I've been done in by that gallows-fodder! That was no carpenter! It was Goosy Gander! And he threatened to come and beat me up twice more!'

Well, well, thought the axe-men. So the cruel Squire had come to grief! So much the worse for him! Good old Goosy Gander! But they didn't say a word because they were afraid of the Squire. Instead, they put him in a sheet and carted him back to his home. The Squire went straight to bed and stayed there because he ached in every bone of his body and he was frightened to death. He asked for letters to be sent to various doctors to come and cure him: but everybody was so afraid of him that not even the doctors dared to come and undertake the task. Within a few days, however, Goosy Gander heard of the Squire's plight too, and he had another idea.

He dressed up as a learned doctor, hired a carriage and drove to Dobrog. He put up at the Inn and made himself known as a doctor from foreign parts. He chatted with the innkeeper for a while and then asked, 'Well, what's the news in this town?'

'Nothing much,' the other replied, 'except that the Squire is mortally ill. I hear that if only some doctor could be found to cure him he would be payed handsomely.'

Goosy stroked his false beard for a while. 'Well,' he said at last, 'I think I'll be able to cure him myself.'

So the innkeeper sent word to the Squire's house that a foreign doctor was at the inn who said that he could cure the Squire. Sure enough, a coach was sent for Goosy and he went up to see his patient.

'Do you think you can cure me?' asked the Squire in a tremulous voice.

'Yes, I think so,' replied Goosy, his spectacles glinting.

He ordered that a fire be lit in the grate, that a hot bath be prepared and that the servants should go out and gather all the medicinal herbs and roots they could find in the forest.

The servants promptly obeyed and left the house. The only people who remained were the doctor and his patient. That was the moment Goosy had been waiting for. He took a strong stick and, swishing it in the air, he stood in front of the Squire of Dobrog.

'Here comes the cure!' he said – and sure enough, he cured the Squire with that stick there and then. All the Squire could do was to revolve his eyes again in agonized surprise.

'I am no doctor,' said Goosy at last, 'but Goosy Gander!'

He saw some money on the table and he helped himself to six crowns – the price of his geese. Then he added:

'Beware! I've come twice already! I shall come once more!'

When the servants returned at last, laden with herbs and roots, they found the Squire more dead than alive. He could hardly croak when they enquired about the doctor.

'That was no doctor! That was Goosy Gander!'

So that's the way of it, thought the servants! Good old Goosy Gander had dealt with the Squire again! No more than he deserved! But as they were still afraid of him, they did not say a word.

A doctor was eventually found who could cure the Squire. When he got up at last, he went around with a bodyguard in case Goosy Gander should try to visit him again. But, as time passed, he forgot about the danger and went about his cruel business as before. But the people of Dobrog were no longer quite so afraid of him: had the Squire not been made a fool of by Goosy Gander twice already?

Some time later it was market-day again in Dobrog. Goosy thought that it was an appropriate day to visit the Squire for the last time, so he dressed himself up as a horse dealer, obtained a good horse and drove it to the market. There he stood among the other dealers and offered his horse for sale.

Having sold it, he strolled round the market, waiting for the arrival of the Squire of Dobrog. He overheard one of the dealers boasting that his horse was the fastest runner in the whole district. This gave Goosy Gander an idea. He went up to the dealer

'Is that so? Because I am looking for just such a horse. I will buy it, but only if you give me a demonstration ride according to my instructions.'

The dealer agreed and Goosy gave him his special instructions. 'Mount your horse and wait just outside town. When you see the Squire of Dobrog coming along the road in his coach, ride up to him and shout: 'I am Goosy Gander!' But then you had better ride hell for leather if you know what's good for you!'

The dealer agreed, mounted his horse and followed Goosy to the roadside just outside town. There they waited until the big coach arrived. The dealer rode up and, according to his instructions, gave a great shout:

'I am Goosy Gander!'

With which he dug his heels in and galloped down the road in a cloud of dust.

'Quick!' shouted the Squire of Dobrog. 'Coachman! Release the horses and ride with the groom after the blighter! A hundred crowns for catching him! Go!!'

And the coachman mounted one horse and the groom the other and they galloped up the road. The squire remained in the coach by himself watching the chase.

That was the moment that Goosy had been waiting for. He strolled up to the coach swishing his stick, and spoke quietly.

'That wasn't Goosy Gander. But I AM!'

The Squire practically fainted with fright. Goosy repaid him with that stick just the same, for the third and last time.

'Mercy!' croaked the Squire when he had at last found his voice. 'Murder! Robbery! Help!!'

But there was nobody there to help him. At least, nobody among the whole population of Dobrog who had gathered behind Goosy to witness the Squire's final humiliation. Instead, the people began to laugh, and cheer, and shout. They weren't afraid of the Squire of Dobrog any more! He could go and practise his cruelty somewhere else! They would have none of him!

The Squire realized that he was beaten. His lordship of Dobrog had come to an end. So he quietly opened the other door of his coach, stepped down and crept away. He is probably creeping still.

The people cheered and shouldered Goosy Gander as their hero. In good time he became the new Squire of Dobrog, took a wife and lived among his happy people for ever and a day.

The Lazy King

BEYOND the seven Kingdoms and across the wide Ocean, there once lived an old and lazy king. That lazy king was genial and fat, and his subjects loved him. And why not, indeed, for he was so lazy that he never waged war, he never conscripted soldiers and he never levied taxes.

He never did a blessed thing, but idled round the livelong day. As an idler though, he was a master. Hardly had he finished his morning laziness, he began to loaf at midday. Then it was time to dawdle in the afternoon, and then in the evening. After that, it was time for his morning laziness again.

As a result of this vast inactivity the Lazy King became so fat that one day, when he wished to leave his bedroom, he found that he could not squeeze through the door.

'Well, let it be so,' said the Lazy King, and he never left his bedroom again.

In fact, within his royal bedroom, the indolence felt even better. He got fatter and fatter until, one day, he realized that he had grown into his room. In other words, whatever free space there had been in the room was now filled out by his own fat royal body. It was just as well that he poked a hole through the ceiling with his head: thus, he obtained some air. Otherwise, he would have choked in a nasty way. Even the laziest of kings need air to breathe.

Henceforth the Lazy King lived thus, with his body in the bedroom and his head in the attic. And it was in the attic that his ministers and his nobles visited him.

'Your Majesty,' said the Prime Minister one day, 'I wish to say something without giving offence.'

The Lazy King bade him speak, and the Prime Minister spoke:

'Your Majesty is mortal too, and it would be a wise thing to decide which of your sons should become the heir to the throne.'

The Lazy King had three sons. He commanded that the Prime Minister should call them to the attic to find out which was the laziest. He would be the one who would then become the future king.

The Prime Minister sounded the trumpet for the three princes. He could have trumpeted 'til Doomsday because none of them made a move, they were all so lazy. Therefore, they had to be placed in sedan-chairs and taken into the presence of their royal father.

'Let us see,' said the King to his eldest son. 'How lazy are you, my son?'

'I am so lazy,' said the eldest son, 'that I will not even close my eyes to go to sleep.'

The Lazy King made a face: 'What sort of an idler is he who cannot even sleep? You will not make a king!'

Then he asked his younger son, 'Let us see, my son, how lazy are you?'

'I am so very lazy,' replied the younger son, 'that when they pour drink into my mouth I am too idle to swallow it.'

The Lazy King made a face: 'He who will not swallow a drink that is poured into his mouth is not lazy but crazy. You will not make a king, either.'

Then it was the turn of the youngest son: 'Let us see, my son, how lazy you are.'

'I am so very, very lazy,' replied the youngest son, 'that when they put food into my mouth, I will not eat it because I am too idle to chew!'

The Lazy King made a face: 'You are foolish, my son, not lazy. He who does not eat dies, and he who is dead will never make a king.'

With that the Lazy King dismissed his sons. When they were gone the Prime Minister asked:

'Your Majesty, who will be our future king?'

'I shall,' replied the Lazy King, 'because my laziness is so frightfully, so awfully, and so immensely vast that I am too lazy even to die.'

And neither did the Lazy King die for another seven hundred and forty-seven years. But then a wasp settled on his nose. The King was too lazy to brush it off and the wasp stung the King's nose. This made the King give such a mighty kick that the palace collapsed on top of him.

If you don't believe it, look under the ruins.

The Joking Wolf

O NCE upon a time there was a mean old peasant. He
owned three animals: a horse, a sow and a goat. But
he was so mean that he begrudged the very food his
animals ate. Indeed, he gave them so little to eat that by
springtime the poor beasts were no better than mere bags
of bones.

So the mean old peasant opened the gate one morning
and shouted angrily at them: 'Get out! You are only fit for
the wolves! Why didn't you fatten up during the winter?'

The poor animals would have gladly fattened up, had
they only been given enough to eat.

A wolf happened to be lurking around the house just
then and he saw the horse coming through the gate. He
was a hungry wolf, so he skipped across and addressed the
horse:

'Let me eat you! After all, your master intended you for
me!'

'If you want to eat me,' replied the horse, 'do so by all

164

means. But I doubt if you'll get much pleasure from it. I am a mere bag of bones. However, I am just about to go up into the hills where I shall graze throughout the summer. I shall become so fat that, when I return, every mouthful you take will be a delight.'

The wolf saw the point and allowed the horse to go on his way. Just then the sow came through the gate. The wolf stopped her:

'Let me eat you! After all, your master intended you for me!'

'I don't mind,' replied the sow, 'but what would you find to eat here? Can't you see that I am just a bag of bones? But if you wait until autumn I shall become so fat up there in the hills, and I shall return with six such succulent piglets that you will have no reason to complain.'

So the wolf allowed the sow to go on her way, too. Just then the goat came out and the wolf skipped across:

'Let me eat you,' he said, 'because after all, your master intended you for me!'

'You can if you must,' replied the goat, 'but I am just a bag of bones. Now if you could only wait until the autumn! I shall be so fat after a whole summer's grazing up in the hills that you will have a real feast.'

The wolf appreciated the logic of this argument and allowed the goat to go on his way too.

During the whole of that summer the wolf prepared himself for the great autumnal feast to come. He dreamt of fat horses, round goats, porky sows and succulent piglets, and as he dreamt he kept licking his lips.

Autumn came at last. The hungry wolf hid himself behind a bush and waited. He whiled away the time trying to guess who would turn up first and he smacked his lips awhile. At last he saw that the sow was trotting down the hillside. She was certainly fat enough now! And sure enough, six succulent little piglets were duly trotting behind her. The wolf skipped out and placed himself in front of the sow.

'You are an honest animal for not playing a trick on me,' he said. 'But come, let me eat you now because I've spent the whole summer keeping my appetite for you.'

'If I wanted to play a trick on you,' replied the sow reprovingly, 'I wouldn't have come down this road. However, there's trouble and you must wait for just one more day.'

'Trouble? What trouble?' demanded the wolf impatiently.

'You see,' explained the sow, 'there was no priest up in the hills. Consequently my six little piglets have not been baptized. Therefore, should you eat them in their present unbaptized state, the poor little creatures won't go to Heaven. And I am sure you wouldn't want that to happen! So, my friend, wait for just another day.'

The wolf couldn't bring himself to condemn the six little piglets to eternal damnation through his own greed. So he told the sow to take her piglets to the priest and have them baptized, but that she must return immediately afterwards because he was getting extremely hungry.

'Thank you, my friend,' said the sow. 'Meanwhile, you might be interested to know the baptismal names of my piglets. So just bend down and lend me an ear, so that I may whisper them to you.'

The wolf bent down accordingly. But, to his horror, the sow caught him by the ear with her teeth and shook him and shook him until he had to cry for mercy. 'Stop it! Stop it! I was only joking!' But the sow went on shaking him and the piglets joined in too, until they shook him nearly out of his skin. In the end the wolf managed to wriggle free and was lucky to escape with his life!

He had hardly had time to recover his breath from the terrible shaking when the goat appeared on the road leading down from the hills. Evidently he hadn't wasted his time up there either, because he was as fat and round as a drum. Seeing him come down the wolf forgot his recent experience, and his mouth began to water.

'Welcome, my friend,' he greeted the goat. 'I am glad to see you so fit and ready to be eaten. But mind you don't play a trick on me like that old sow!'

'Why should I play a trick on you?' protested the goat in a hurt voice. 'Didn't I eat my way diligently through the whole of the summer so that you could have a satisfying meal?'

'You are an honest animal,' said the wolf, slobbering, 'and I am very grateful. As a reward I shall eat you gently.'

'I am so glad,' replied the goat, 'because I meant to ask you to spare me any unnecessary pain. To do this, could you perhaps swallow me whole, without any chewing?'

The wolf nodded his assent. Whereupon the goat asked the wolf to throw his head back and open his mouth as wide as possible so that he could jump neatly down his throat. The wolf did as he was told. The goat then lowered his head, ran up and charged. He butted so hard that the wolf fell in a daze and rolled over and over. The goat followed him and butted him again and again before running home.

'I was only joking!' croaked the wolf, in case the goat came back to butt him yet again. When he was sure that the goat had gone he picked himself up painfully and crawled behind a bush. He had hardly recovered from his second ordeal when he heard hoofbeats and saw that the horse was coming down the road. The sight cheered him up considerably. No bag of bones there either, thought the wolf licking his lips, but a big fat morsel for his dinner!

'I am so glad you've arrived,' said the wolf in greeting, 'but mind you don't play a trick on me like the sow or the goat! I need my dinner!'

'Do you really think I'd have come down this road if I wanted to play a trick on you?' The horse was plainly offended.

'Come here then,' encouraged the wolf in a wheedling manner, 'so that I may eat you, munch-munch!'

'You may certainly eat me munch-munch,' replied the horse, 'but there's a wedding in the village and I have to carry the bride to church first. When I've done my job I'll come back to be eaten.'

Oh no you don't, thought the wolf. He wouldn't let the horse out of his sight in case he played a trick on him too. He told the horse that he too would come and see the bride for himself.

'All right,' replied the horse, 'come with me. I'll carry you on my back.'

The wolf mounted and the horse cantered towards the village. Sure enough a wedding was being prepared and the whole population was assembled in front of the church. When they suddenly saw a cantering horse with a wolf sitting on its back they began to shout: 'The mounted wolf is here! The mounted wolf is here!'

With that the men grabbed shovels, mattocks, hoes and rods and fell upon the hapless wolf who began crying for mercy. 'Stop it! Stop it! I was only joking!' But the men thrashed and whacked and walloped him so soundly that he could hardly crawl back into the forest.

A woodman happened to be digging in the forest just then. He heard that almighty hullabaloo from the village and looked out to see what was amiss. But when he saw a panting wolf loping towards him he was so frightened that he hid himself behind a tree. The wolf was afraid, too, lest the men from the village should chase after him, so he hid behind the same tree. But on the other side of it.

He remained there for a while, licking his wounds. Then he sighed bitterly and moaned, 'It serves me right for being so stupid! I deserve to be thumped over the head for my folly!'

'Well if that's what you want,' said the woodman — and he hit the wolf over the head, thump!

'But I was only joking!' cried the wolf in alarm as he jumped up and ran away deep into the forest. What's the world coming to, he pondered, when people can't even take a joke any more?

The Obstinate Little Rabbit

ONCE upon a time there was an obstinate little rabbit. This obstinate little rabbit had a silver-tinkling little bell round his neck. Every time the little rabbit took a step, the little bell tinkled, just as every time he didn't take a step, the little bell didn't tinkle.

One day his brother-in-law invited the little rabbit to lunch and entertained him properly. On his way home the obstinate little rabbit realized that he had eaten far too much because his stomach was dragging along the ground. He looked around for a suitable spot where he could doze for a while, at least until his stomach subsided a bit. At the edge of the wood he saw a little bush, so he hung his silver-tinkling bell upon it and he settled himself on the grass beneath. Soon he was fast asleep.

When he woke up next morning he looked this way and that for the little bush, but it was nowhere to be seen: instead, he saw a slender tree in its place. And there, on its topmost branch, was the little silver bell. The stubborn little rabbit addressed the tall tree:

'Look here, slender tree, give me back my silver bell!'

The slender tree replied, 'No I won't. Why should I? It suits me well too.'

'Let me not be called an obstinate little rabbit if you don't give it back!' said the little rabbit and he ran and he ran until he reached the axe.

'Look here, axe,' he said, 'go to the slender tree, ask for the silver bell and if he doesn't give it back, cut him down.'

Whereupon the axe replied, 'Why should I? I have other work to do.'

'Let me not be called an obstinate little rabbit if you don't do as I say!' said the little rabbit and he ran and he ran until he reached the rock.

'Look here, rock,' he said, 'go to the axe, send the axe to the slender tree, and if he won't go, blunt his edge.'

Whereupon the rock replied, 'Why should I? I have other work to do.'

'Let me not be called an obstinate little rabbit if you don't do as I say!' replied the little rabbit and he ran and he ran until he reached the bull.

'Look here, bull,' he said, 'go to the rock, send the rock to the axe; if he won't go, roll him into the water!'

Whereupon the bull replied, 'Why should I? I have other work to do!'

'Let me not be called an obstinate little rabbit if you don't do as I say!' said the little rabbit and he ran and he ran until he reached the bee.

'Look here, bee,' he said, 'go to the bull, send the bull to the rock, and if he won't go, sting him hard!'

Whereupon the bee replied. 'Why should I? I have other work to do!'

'Let me not be called an obstinate little rabbit if you don't do as I say!' said the little rabbit and he ran and he ran until he reached the crow.

'Look here, crow,' he said, 'go to the bee, send the bee to the bull, and if he won't go, swallow him at once!'

Whereupon the crow replied, 'Why should I? I have other work to do!'

'Let me not be called an obstinate little rabbit if you don't do as I say!' said the little rabbit and he ran and he ran until he reached the cat.

'Look here, cat,' he said, 'go to the crow, send the crow to the bee, and if he won't go, wring his neck!'

Whereupon the cat replied, 'I would do so willingly, but I haven't eaten for two days and I can hardly move. Bring me a little milk and I will do as you say.'

Just then a servant came by, carrying a pail of milk. The obstinate little rabbit gave a great cry: 'Wolf! A wolf! Here comes the wolf!' The servant slammed down the pail and ran away. The obstinate little rabbit took the pail to the cat. The cat drank the milk and went to face the crow.

'Look here, crow,' he said, 'go to the bee and send the bee to the bull, or I'll wring your neck!'

Whereupon the crow replied, 'I am going, I am going, of course I'll go and do as you say!' And he went to face the bee.

'Look here, bee,' he said, 'go to the bull and send the bull to the rock, or I'll swallow you at once!'

Whereupon the bee replied, 'I am going, I am going, of course I'll go and do as you say!' And he went to face the bull.

'Look here, bull,' he said, 'go to the rock and send the rock to the axe, or I'll sting you hard!'

Whereupon the bull replied, 'I am going, I am going, of course I'll go and do as you say!' And he went to face the rock.

'Look here, rock,' he said, 'go to the axe and send the axe to the slender tree, or I'll roll you into the water!'

Whereupon the rock replied, 'I am going, I am going, of course I'll go and do as you say!' And he went to face the axe.

'Look here, axe,' he said, 'go to the slender tree and ask for the silver bell, or I'll blunt your edge!'

Whereupon the axe replied, 'I am going, I am going, of course I'll go and do as you say!' And he went to face the slender tree.

'Look here, slender tree,' he said, 'give back the silver bell, or I'll cut you down!'

When the slender tree saw the axe he was so frightened that he trembled in every branch and twig. All that trembling made the little silver bell on the topmost branch tinkle. And it continued to tinkle-jingle, jingle-tinkle, until the slender tree dropped it, and it fell at the feet of the obstinate little rabbit.

'You see, you did give it back to me after all!' said the obstinate little rabbit as he hung the silver-tinkling little bell round his neck.

And he has been wearing it round his neck ever since.

Sammy Lazybones

ONCE upon a time there was a couple who lived on their big farm. They had been married for a very long time but they had no children. At long last, one fine day, their patience was rewarded by the birth of their son Sammy. They were both old by then, so you can imagine how delighted they were to have a son at last. They petted and pampered and spoiled him the live-long day: he was the apple of their old eyes.

If he moaned once, his mother ran to see, if he moaned twice, they both ran. If he cried, the doctor was called and came running. When he was hungry they fed him. When

175

he refused they entreated him to eat. If he resisted they both cried oh misery, what will become of you, you'll shrivel up, the wind will blow you away!

And when it blew they covered him up. When the sun shone they put him in the shade. Was it raining? They put up an umbrella for him. Did he yawn? They prepared his bed. There was nothing they would not do for him.

Sammy became so used to his pampered life that eventually he hardly bothered to open his mouth. When he was hungry he just pointed to his stomach and that was enough for the old couple. They ran for food. One of them would hold Sammy's head while the other fed him by the spoonful. They cut up his meat to save him from chewing. Afterwards they undressed him and put him to bed. In the morning they washed him and combed his hair. He was a big lad by then, yet he had never been anywhere beyond his own backyard. As for doing any work, he had never done a stroke. A sick flea would have done more.

But, one day, his old father died.

Sammy was sad but he could hardly cry, it was such an effort. His old mother kept on looking after him. She was weak and feeble by then, yet she fetched and carried for him all day long. She fetched and carried for so long that she became weaker and feebler still until, finally, she gave up her soul too.

So, one day, Sammy found himself all alone in the house. And he was hungry. So he yelled. The neighbour came running to see what was amiss. He found Sammy stretched on his bed, still yelling.

'What ails you, Sammy Lazybones?' he enquired.

'I am hungry!' complained Sammy.

Well, thought the good neighbour, the poor lad was in mourning so he might as well bring him some food to cheer him up. But was that enough for Sammy? Oh no. As soon as he had eaten his fill Sammy began to order his neighbour around. That he should bring in some water. That he should wash him. That he should make his bed.

The neighbour was a good man and did as he was told. But before he returned to his own house he spoke to Sammy:

'I am sorry for you because you are in mourning, but don't suppose that I shall be your servant. From now on you must look after yourself. You are old enough after all.'

'Very well,' agreed Sammy — yet by next morning he broke into the most fearful lamentations again, as if he had been skinned alive and salted and peppered to boot.

The neighbour heard those dreadful sounds and promptly forgot what had happened the previous day. So he came running again. He found Sammy still stretched on his bed, yelling his head off.

'What ails you this time, Sammy Lazybones?' asked the neighbour.

'I am hungry and thirsty,' complained Sammy petulantly.

The neighbour was upset at the thought that Sammy had taken him in again, but he was a good-natured man. So he brought some food in from the larder, washed Sammy and tidied up his bed. But he warned him that it was no good yelling out again because he would not come next time.

Sammy promised faithfully that he would look after himself from now on and that he would not disturb his neighbour again.

Promises, just promises. Because next day the good neighbour heard the most terrible yammering and caterwauling again from Sammy's house. He thought that the wretched boy must have been attacked by robbers this time and he came running to help.

But there were no robbers in Sammy's house. Only Sammy — still stretched on his bed, still yammering.

'What's up now?' asked the neighbour, a little impatiently.

'I am so fearfully hungry,' croaked Sammy, 'that if you don't get me some food I won't last 'til nightfall!'

'Now look here, Sammy Lazybones,' said the neighbour, who had just about had enough, 'this won't do. I have enough work of my own. I will not fetch and carry for you any more!'

'Do you want me to perish in front of your eyes?' wailed Sammy.

'No,' replied the neighbour, 'but I will tell you what you must do if you don't want to perish.'

'What?' asked Sammy.

'Marry.'

'Me?' Sammy was incredulous. 'Marry? Everybody knows what a lazybones I am. I don't know a single girl hereabouts who would be foolish enough to marry me!'

'But I do,' replied the neighbour. 'And she is far from foolish either — she is very clever, in fact. But poor.'

Sammy sat up. He became interested. He asked about the girl. Was she dark or fair? Fat or thin? Tall or short? He heard that her name was Juliska. That she was the daughter of the swineherd. That they lived at the end of the village. Having heard all he wanted to know, Sammy said:

'Very well, neighbour, in that case I'll accept your advice. Go and tell Juliska that she may come any time. I'll marry her.'

Saying which he lay back on his bed again.

This was too much for the neighbour. Anger flooded him. He went red in the face. His eyes revolved in their sockets. He looked round for something to smash. He found a cup – he smashed it against the wall. He found a jug – he smashed it against the table. He found a dish – he smashed that too. He managed to calm down a little after that. Sufficiently, that is, to say what he had to say.

'Now look here, Lazybones! This is the end. If you are so infernally lazy that you won't even go to ask the girl yourself then I will have nothing to do with you any more! I don't care if you starve to death because you asked for it!'

Saying which he stalked out of the house. He slammed the door so hard behind him that three china mugs (which he forgot to smash earlier) fell off the shelf and broke to smithereens.

So Sammy Lazybones was left alone – his only companions were hunger and thirst. He didn't know which was the worst. He tried yelling again, howling for help. But it was no good this time because his neighbour stuffed his ears with bread and couldn't hear a thing. There was only one thing to be done, Sammy decided. It was a terrible decision to make, but he made it. He would get up.

The very thought made him groan. He groaned for a good hour before he managed to heave himself into a sitting position. He groaned for another hour before he managed to place his feet on the floor. However, by that time he was so hungry that with a final groan he stood up and staggered straight towards the larder.

But the larder was empty. The shelves were empty. The bins were empty. The sacks were empty. Not a sausage anywhere.

This frightened Sammy Lazybones so much that he even forgot his laziness. He was terrified that he would die in the empty larder. He was so alarmed at the prospect that without a further thought or a single groan he marched out of the house, down the village road and he didn't stop until he reached the swineherd's house. There he knocked.

'Welcome to our house,' said the swineherd when he opened the door.

'Welcome to our house,' said Juliska, the swineherd's daughter.

They made him sit down and offered him cake and some wine. Sammy ate and drank, but for the life of him he could not think of anything to say. The very effort made him break into a sweat. His lifelong laziness had made his brain lazy, too. So he just sat there until nightfall, without uttering a single word. Then he got up to take his leave and the swineherd escorted him to the gate and asked him to come again and said that he would be welcome.

The neighbour saw Sammy return to his house and asked how he had fared at the swineherd's.

'Well enough,' replied Sammy, 'but only her father escorted me out.'

'Go again tomorrow,' advised the neighbour.

So Sammy went again. He received the same polite welcome, he was made to sit down again and they offered him food and drink. And all the while Sammy cudgelled his brains for something to say but he couldn't think of anything. So at nightfall he stood up and took his leave. This time it was the swineherd's wife who saw him to the gate and asked him to come again.

'How did it go this time?' enquired the neighbour when Sammy got home.

'Well enough,' said he, 'but only her mother saw me out this time.'

'Go again tomorrow,' urged his neighbour.

So off he went for the third time. He sat down, ate and drank, but said not a word. Not a single solitary word until nightfall. When he stood up to take his leave the swineherd's wife spoke to her daughter:

'Juliska, my dear, go and escort our guest to the gate.'

Juliska agreed obediently. They walked to the gate and, at long last, Sammy Lazybones remembered that he had an important question to ask.

'Do you know, Juliska, why I have come three times to your house?'

'I shall know when you tell me.'

'I came,' announced Sammy, 'because I want to marry you.'

'Sir, please do not mock me!'

'I am not mocking! I want to marry you straight away.'

'Well, if you are serious,' replied Juliska modestly, 'I must first ask my father and mother if they approve.'

So Sammy went home and the girl returned to the house to ask her parents.

'He would make a good husband,' said the swineherd, 'because he has much land and many animals. But he won't do a stroke of work himself, and if you married him you would have to work your fingers to the bone.'

'Leave that to me, Father,' said Juliska, with a smile.

When Sammy told his neighbour that Juliska seemed willing to marry him it was decided that, as it was customary, they should both call at the swineherd's house next day to ask for Juliska's hand.

Accordingly they called. The swineherd received them formally, they asked for Juliska's hand on Sammy's behalf and the swineherd consented. The marriage was announced and, in proper time, duly solemnized.

Juliska moved into Sammy's house and life continued as before. To be more precise, Sammy spent his days in slothful indolence lying on his bed, and Juliska spent hers seeing to all his needs and doing all the other work besides.

Until the summer, that is. It was then that she spoke:

'The corn is ripe and we shall go to harvest it.'

'It is all the same to me,' replied Sammy, 'as long as you bring a chair.'

Off to the meadow they went, sickles and chair and all. Juliska placed the chair at the edge of the cornfield and Sammy slumped into it, stretched out his legs and surveyed the scene in comfort. She, meanwhile, took her sickle and got down to work. She laboured and toiled under the hot sun until the midday bells were sounded. Then she spoke to her husband.

'Stay here while I go back to fetch the dinner. Our neighbour's good wife has baked us a pie.'

'Hurry up then,' he urged her, 'because I am famished.'

Juliska hurried back to the village, secretly amused awhile at the lesson she would give her husband. The neighbour's son was a soldier and he was at home on leave. Juliska spoke to him:

'Gallant sir, if you would be so kind may I borrow your uniform for a while?'

The soldier gave it to her. She put it on, buckled the sword to her side and pencilled a moustache under her nose so that Sammy should not recognize her. Thus equipped she went straight back to the cornfield.

'Good day!' she greeted Sammy. 'May I enquire what you are doing here sitting on that chair?'

'I am waiting for my wife, sir soldier,' said he.

'And why are you waiting for your wife?' pursued the soldier.

'To bring me a pie because I am hungry, and to move my chair into the shade because I am hot.'

The soldier surveyed Sammy with narrowed eyes, just like a horse-dealer inspecting a broken old nag.

'Don't you do any harvesting, then?'

'No, because I don't know how to.'

The soldier's eyes sparked. The sword flew out of its scabbard and it flashed in front of Sammy's nose. He was so alarmed that it nearly made him sneeze.

'W-what d-do you want, s-sir soldier?' stammered Sammy in sheer terror.

'I will teach you to harvest.'

'B-but my wife does all the harvesting here!'

'Does she now?' sneered the soldier. No matter. Sammy was ordered to pick up his sickle and get down to work. He protested and begged to be left in peace, but that wicked sword was still flashing under his nose. So what could he do? He took up the sickle and began to work in a half-hearted manner.

'Faster!' commanded the soldier. 'Faster!' And with each command the flat of that sword thwacked smartly down on Sammy's back. He was chased round the cornfield thus until less than half the corn was left standing.

'Very well,' said the soldier at last, sheathing the sword. 'I am off now, but I shall soon return. And mark this. If I don't find you hard at work, I will cut off your nose first, your ears next and your head last. Is that understood?'

The soldier marched off and returned to the neighbour's house to unbuckle the sword, take off the uniform, wash off the moustache and change back into Juliska once more. Then she thanked the neighbour's soldier-son for his help, took the pie from the neighbour's good wife and returned to the cornfield.

Half the village had assembled there meanwhile, because news had spread that Sammy was at work. They were amazed at such a sight. They could hardly believe what they saw. Sammy was working so fast that it almost hurt the eye trying to keep up with him.

'What are you doing, husband?' called Juliska. 'You weren't working when I left you.'

'But I am working now sure enough,' he called back.

'What came over you to do such a thing?' she enquired.

'Nothing, except that a fierce soldier came this way and threatened to cut off my nose and ears and head if I didn't. So I thought I'd rather work.'

And without another word he resumed his task. You could hardly see his sickle it went so fast and soon the whole of the corn had been harvested. What's more, he didn't even touch the pie until supper that night!

The truth was that Sammy was mightily afraid of the fierce soldier and his flashing sword. Did he not say that he would soon return? And if not today, might he not return tomorrow or next week or next year? Sammy thought that flashing swords were dangerous things and he was far too fond of his nose and his ears and his head.

So ever since then there is nobody in the whole of the village who works as hard as Sammy. And when he remembers the soldier he works twice as hard. Juliska just smiles and bakes him a pie to cheer him up, and she is glad that nobody calls him Lazybones any more.

Briar Peter

ONCE upon a time there was a boy who lived with his father. He also had a stepmother and she was a most spiteful woman who annoyed and scolded young Peter all the livelong day. Every time he was out of doors she called him in; whenever he was indoors, she sent him out, and all the time she cursed him with bell, book and candle. She begrudged him the very food and drink he ate and drank.

Peter was, therefore, very surprised one day when his stepmother actually set a plate of potato soup in front of him. But as he was very hungry he sat down straight away and took up his spoon. As he opened his mouth for the first spoonful of soup he saw, out of the corner of his eye, a branch of the briar bush poking its way through the window towards him! The bush had been planted outside the window by his own dear mother and when the branch began to speak, Peter's mouth remained open in astonishment.

'My dearest boy,' said the branch, 'do not eat your soup. It is poisoned! Leave the house, and for your own safety, go away!'

Peter closed his mouth and dropped his spoon. He got up and, without saying a word, left the house for ever. He walked fast and he dared not stop in case his stepmother came after him. Much later, as he walked along the bank of a stream, someone called him by name:

'Peter, Peter, Briar Peter, come here!'

He saw a poor little fish writhing in the grass, hardly able to breathe. 'Throw me into the stream, Briar Peter. Your good deed will be rewarded one day!'

The boy threw him in and the little fish swam away joyfully. Peter went on his way. That night he met some shepherds who gave him warm milk and soft bread to eat.

Next morning he was on his way again when, once more, he heard someone call his name:

'Peter, Peter, Briar Peter, come here!'

This time it was a little bird lying on the ground, evidently too young to fly. He asked Peter to lift him up into a tree. Peter put him on a branch and, as he went his way, he heard the little bird call after him:

'Your good deed will be rewarded one day!'

He journeyed on, going up hill and down dale, wherever the road led him.

He travelled aimlessly for many days like this, until, one day, he heard a call yet again:

'Peter, Peter, Briar Peter, come here!'

He looked and, to his delight, he saw that this time it was a briar bush which called for help. The poor bush was withering away for lack of water. Peter ran to find a brook, filled his hat with fresh spring water and returned to sprinkle the roots of the little bush. It began to recover straight away and soon its leaves were bright green and full of renewed vigour.

'Your good deed will be rewarded one day!' said the briar.

'I was not thinking of a reward,' replied Peter shyly.

'All the same,' said the bush, 'I shall give you some advice. It is this: have no fear when danger comes near; your good fortune is found where the worst of threats abound.'

How strange, thought Peter, that he should go and seek danger and threats in order to find his good fortune! But he continued on his journey with real purpose now and he walked with a spring in his step. He kept looking around for signs of human life and, whenever he saw the smoke of a chimney, he made for it straight away. He knocked on every door and entered every inn and he mixed with soldiers and brigands in order to provoke a quarrel. But all to no avail. He came to no harm anywhere and nobody threatened or menaced him. He wanted to meet danger because he longed to find his good fortune.

One day he came to a big city, and he made for the royal palace straight away. There was a crowd of people at the gate and when they saw Peter they came running and shouting:

'Come here, come here, Briar Peter! Ninety-nine have gone to the gallows before you and you will be the hundredth!'

'At last,' thought Peter, 'I've come to the right place for

danger! I'll find my good fortune here if I find it anywhere! But how?' Fortunately, the major-domo of the palace came out just then and told Peter that he must come and face a test.

It seemed that the King had a daughter. She decided one day to get married. The King agreed and sent for a dozen princes so that she could make her choice. But the stubborn Princess refused to accept any of them. So the King ordered three dozen dukes. The Princess didn't want any of those, either. Neither did she want any of the earls or viscounts.

The King had lost patience by then.

'If you refuse to marry anybody whom you have seen with your own eyes,' growled the King, 'you must marry somebody whom you have not. Let me tell you this. As from now, you shall only marry a man who can hide himself three times in succession and whom you can't find. If you do find him every time, he must go to the gallows!'

The Princess burst into tears. Had she tried to pick and choose amongst all those princes, dukes, earls and viscounts only to marry a man whom she had never seen? But the King was adamant. He advertised the conditions and ninety-nine applicants came forward and failed the test. And Briar Peter had now come forward as the hundredth.

They led him into the palace and gave him all the food and drink he wanted. They treated him as they might have treated a condemned man. They kept badgering him to take more of this and that. Eventually, they left him alone so that he could work out a good hiding place for the morrow.

Peter spent the whole night in thought. He might as well have gone to bed instead, because he was quite incapable of thinking of anything, and sleep would have done him more good. Next morning they came to tell him that he must go and hide himself before midday.

Peter wandered around sadly without having an idea for a good hiding-place, when he came to a river. He sat down and wept, watering the river with his tears.

'Peter, Peter, Briar Peter, why are you weeping?'

Peter looked up and saw that it was the little fish whom he had thrown back into the stream some while before. He told the fish why he was so sad.

'Your good deed is now rewarded,' replied the fish. He opened his mouth and urged Peter to climb in. Peter did so and the fish jumped back into the river, swam downstream and hid in the sand at the bottom of the sea.

At midday the Princess came out on the porch, rubbed her eyes and said:

'Come forth, Briar Peter, come forth from the mouth of the fish that hides in the sand at the bottom of the sea!'

What could he do? He climbed out and strolled dejectedly back to the palace. In his sadness he was unaware that the beautiful Princess had taken a secret glance in his direction.

Come the next morning, Peter found himself just as incapable of working out a good hiding-place as on the morning before. By the side of the palace there was a pleasant wood and Peter made his way there to weep and ruminate. Suddenly, he heard a voice again:

'Peter, Peter, Briar Peter, why are you weeping?'

Peter looked up and saw that it was the same little bird whom he had lifted up and placed on a branch some time before.

'I weep,' replied Peter, 'because if I can't find a place to hide from the Princess, the King will send me to the gallows.'

'Your good deed is now rewarded,' said the bird. He

spread his wings and told Peter to hide himself beneath
them. Then, the bird flew up and up, and hid behind the
sun.

At midday the Princess came out again, rubbed her eyes
twice and said:

'Come forth, Briar Peter, come forth from beneath the
wings of the bird who hides behind the sun.'

The little bird brought Peter down and placed him at
the side of the Princess. She took another secret glance at
him. Her look was filled with such tenderness and longing
that it would have melted the heart of a stone. But Peter's
eyes remained downcast in his sorrow.

The third morning had arrived. By now Peter had lost
heart. Why should he attempt to find a hiding-place since
the Princess could find him even at the bottom of the sea,
or at the back of the sun? He would rather stay where he
was without hiding, in the palace garden.

But just then he heard a voice:

'Peter, Peter, Briar Peter, why are you weeping?'

He looked up and saw it was a briar bush. Whether it
was the briar bush that bloomed outside the window at
home, or the briar bush whom he revived with a hatful of
water, it spoke:

'I know what is troubling you, my son. Come, I will
help you.'

The briar bush placed itself in front of the porch and let
down its roots. Peter hid among its branches, whereupon
the bush blossomed out with so many new leaves and roses
that it would have gladdened the heart of anyone who saw
it.

At midday the Princess came out on the porch again.
She took heed of the seas, the countries, the mountains and
the sky, but she saw no sign of Peter.

'I do not see him, father,' she said.

'You don't see him because you have not rubbed your eyes!'

So she rubbed her eyes once, she rubbed them twice. And she did see Peter this time, hiding among the flowers of the briar bush. But she said not a word. She knew only too well that if she did, Peter would go to the gallows. She loved him too much and she wanted him more than she wanted anyone else in the world. Therefore, she rubbed her eyes for a third time, looked all around the earth and the sky and called in a heart-rending voice:

'Peter, Peter, Briar Peter, come forth from wherever you are! Come forth, I cannot see you and my heart is breaking!'

Peter did not wait for a third command: he sprang from the briar bush, bounded up the steps of the porch and took the Princess in his arms. They were married that very day.

And the garden of the palace is now planted with briar bushes from end to end.